BROMSGROVE BOOKSELLER

A captivating Victorian historical murder mystery

KERRY TOMBS

Inspector Ravenscroft Detective Mysteries Book 9

JOFFE BOOKS

First published 2020
Joffe Books, London
www.joffebooks.com

ISBN 978-1-78931-560-8

PROLOGUE

LEDBURY, 21 DECEMBER 1892

'I do believe that we shall have a white Christmas,' said Inspector Ravenscroft, staring out of the window of his cottage in Church Lane. He was watching an old man making his slow way up the cobbled lane, a parcel under his arm. The fellow paused briefly under a sputtering gas lamp, then resumed his course.

'You said that last year,' replied his wife, without looking up from the book she was reading. 'It was so warm we had to have the window open on Christmas afternoon.'

'Yes, I do remember, but I really think that it will snow this year. It certainly looks very cold and inhospitable out there this evening. I shall be more than glad to remain indoors tonight.'

'I don't mind if it snows. In fact, I think I would quite like it,' said Lucy. 'Christmas is rather special when it snows. There is something quite pleasant in sitting by the fireside after a hearty meal, in the company of people that you love, looking out on a snowy winter scene.'

Ravenscroft smiled as he resumed his seat by the fireside.

'I just hope that you are not called out on Christmas Day to solve some ghastly murder, in a remote part of the Three Counties.'

'More likely I will be summoned to break up a drunken dispute in the Market Place between the Leewood family and their associates.'

'At least that would require you to remain in Ledbury.'

'And still be home in time for the goose!' laughed Ravenscroft. He removed his spectacles and began to clean them on his handkerchief.

'I am so looking forward to Richard coming home from school tomorrow,' said Lucy. 'It will be nice for us all to be together again at Christmas, and for Richard to play with his little brother, Arthur.'

'Indeed. I know you have missed him a great deal since we sent him to Dormington.'

'Four months. I am sure I will not recognise him when I see him.'

'He seems to have settled in quite well there, according to his letters. I think it was the right thing for him.'

'I am only thankful that we did not send him to that dreadful school near Bromyard.'

'We certainly had a lucky escape there.' Ravenscroft opened his newspaper.

'Good heavens!' exclaimed Lucy, after a few minutes of silence had elapsed.

'Whatever is the matter?'

'It says here that Olivia Proudie and the Rev. Tobias Tickler went on their honeymoon to Malvern.'

'Really,' muttered Ravenscroft from behind his paper.

'Malvern, of all places,' continued Lucy.

'Why should they not visit Malvern for their honeymoon? There is plenty to do in Malvern, if you like walking in the fresh air, and don't mind the steep hills. Anyway, who is this Olivia Proudie and the Reverend, whatever you said his name was?'

'Tickler. Tobias Tickler.'

'Tickler. Rather an unfortunate name. Do we know these people? I don't recall going to their wedding, and I don't think I have ever encountered people with those names in any of the cases I have been investigating.'

'They are characters in this book I am reading. They don't exist, except in the author's imagination.'

'I see — and who is the author of your book?'

'Anthony Trollope. It is called *Framley Parsonage*; it is one of his Barsetshire novels.'

'I hope it is good?'

'Exceedingly so. If you remember, I gave you this book some time ago. You really should read it, Samuel. You might even like it.'

'How long is it?'

'It is nearly five hundred pages.'

'That is far too long for me. I would never have the time to read such a long book, let alone finish such an undertaking. I much prefer either the local newspaper or *The Strand*.'

'You and your Sherlock Holmes stories,' scoffed Lucy.

'I like Sherlock Holmes. He always solves the case and brings the criminal to justice.'

'Just like you, Samuel!'

'That is not always so, my dear. I can name a number of villains who have escaped justice over the years. Anyway, I am sure that your *Framley Parsonage* must be a big improvement on that other book you were reading last week.'

'Oh, you mean *Frankenstein*.'

'Absolute nonsense,' scoffed Ravenscroft.

'I thought it rather good.'

'Nonsense from beginning to end. As if a man could create a monster by bringing the dead back to life. It was absolute nonsense!'

'I think you should read *A Christmas Carol*, as it is Christmas,' suggested Lucy.

'I read that some years ago. An interesting story, but I did not quite believe in Scrooge's reform of character on

Christmas morning. I don't think you can change from being a miserly old skinflint overnight, if that is your true nature.'

'So you do not believe in redemption?'

'I did not exactly say that,' protested Ravenscroft, aware that he was about to embark on a discussion that he could not possibly win.

'As a policeman you must believe that even the hardest criminal can reform?' continued Lucy.

'As a policeman, it is my job to catch criminals. I leave it to others to reform them.'

'That is rather a pessimistic view to take.'

'Come in!' shouted the detective in response to a knock on the door.

'Excuse me, sir, this letter has just been delivered,' said the maid entering the room.

'Thank you, Susan.' Lucy took the envelope. 'It's addressed to you, Samuel.'

Ravenscroft received the letter and brought it closer to the lamp. 'I don't recognise the handwriting. The envelope is somewhat grubby on the outside, and the hand is rather spidery and indistinct.'

'It must be from one of your admirers,' teased Lucy.

'I don't have any admirers,' replied Ravenscroft, opening the envelope. 'Good Lord, it's from Maisie Stebbins.'

'Maisie Stebbins? Is she related to that young man who came here one evening, two or three years ago?'

'Yes, young Stebbins. He must have married the house servant who worked in that strange lodging house in Pershore. I wonder why she is writing to me?' asked Ravenscroft. He read the letter out loud.

'Dear Inspector Ravenscroft,

I hope you is not minding me writing to you like this, but it is on behalf of my dear Stebbins. Poor Stebbins has got himself into a lot of trouble.

They say he murdered his old Uncle Stebby, and that he will hang for it. I knows he did not, but the police say he did, and have arrested him and put him in Worcester Jail. We don't knows what to do. Stebbins says you is the only one who can help us, and that if ever he got into any kind of trouble I was to get in touch with you.

He did not do it, Inspector Ravenscroft. You has to believe me.

You has to help us.

I hope you don't mind me writing to you like this, but we knows of no one else who can help us like you can.

Yours most humbly,
Maisie Stebbins.'

'It all sounds very serious.' Lucy sounded concerned.

'Yes. I know Stebbins is rather an impetuous and highly imaginative youth, but I cannot see him hurting a fly, let alone murdering his uncle.'

'Then you must go to his assistance.'

'I suppose I must help the poor fellow. Maisie says that they are holding him in Worcester Jail. Tom and I will go over there tomorrow morning and see what this is all about.'

'Can you spare the time?'

'Things are all very quiet at the moment. I am sure that Ledbury can look after itself for one day without my presence.'

'Then you should definitely go and see what you can do for the poor man.'

'Yes,' replied Ravenscroft, placing the letter back in the envelope. 'Well, Stebbins, what kind of trouble have you got yourself into this time?'

CHAPTER ONE

WORCESTER, 22 DECEMBER

Ravenscroft banged his fist heavily against the old wooden studded door. 'Confound it, where is the fellow!'

'Alright, alright, I'm coming,' shouted a voice from the other side.

'Perhaps he has been asleep,' said Sergeant Crabb.

A viewing panel slid back in the door. 'Well, what do you want?' scowled an unshaven, bleary-eyed face.

'Detective Inspector Ravenscroft to see one of your prisoners,' replied the detective in a firm voice.

'Who?'

'Ravenscroft.'

'Never heard of you.' The man began to close the slide.

'Wait!' counteracted Ravenscroft. 'Where is Harris?'

'Dead. Ran out under a carriage near Diglis.'

'I am sorry to hear that.'

'Don't be. The silly old codger should have looked where he was going.'

'And you are?' asked Ravenscroft, ignoring the last remark.

'Smith. I'm jailer here now.'

'Well, Mr Smith, I am Detective Inspector Ravenscroft and this is my colleague, Detective Sergeant Crabb, from Ledbury. We would like a word with one of your prisoners by the name of Stebbins.'

'I've never heard of you. How do I know that you are who you say you are? You could be some criminal mastermind attempting to gain access to the prison, so you can spring one of your associates.'

'I can assure you that we are not members of the criminal fraternity. Here is my identification,' said Ravenscroft, becoming annoyed by the jailer's offhand manner.

'That's no good.'

'Why?'

'Can't read, can I?'

'Then how on earth did you ever secure employment here?'

'They couldn't find anyone else to take it on. This job isn't for those that frighten easy. I comes highly recommended I does.'

'Look here, Smith, this will not do at all.' Ravenscroft raised his voice. 'Either you accept what we say and admit us to the prison, or I will be forced to go to my superintendent here in Worcester and inform him of your conduct. I am sure that your superiors will not be too pleased when they learn of your obstinate and obstructive manner. Which is it to be? May I also remind you that it is a criminal offence to obstruct police officers in the carrying out of their lawful duty.'

'Alright, alright!' protested the jailer, slamming shut the slide, before reluctantly drawing back the bolts on the other side of the door. 'Suppose it won't do no harm,' he muttered as Ravenscroft and Crabb entered the prison. 'Who is it you said you want to see?'

'Young man by the name of Stebbins,' said Crabb.

'Stebbins, you say? He looks a bad one to me.'

'Oh? Why do you say that?' enquired Ravenscroft.

'He's got that look about him. Shifty, if you ask me. I can always tell a bad one when I sees him. They says he murdered his uncle, in cold blood. Knifed him in the back, he did! He is due to stand trial next week. Reckon we will be calling on the services of the hangman quite soon after that. Been some time since we had a hanging here at Worcester,' replied Smith, picking up a large bunch of keys from off the hall table.

'How do you know that?' asked Ravenscroft.

'Know what?'

'That it has been a while since they had a hanging here in Worcester. How do you know that? I thought you said that you had only recently been employed here?'

'I reads the papers, don't I?'

'You told us you could not read,' said Crabb.

'Look, can we get on. We have not got all day to engage in idle chatter. The prisoner Stebbins, if you please, Mr Smith,' instructed Ravenscroft impatiently.

'Best follow me then,' replied the jailer, picking up a lantern and leading the way down a dark dank corridor.

As they passed the cells, Ravenscroft and Crabb heard sounds of crying and shouting from some of the imprisoned inmates.

'Shut up, you old fleabag, or I will come in there and give you one!' cried out Smith, banging on one of the cell doors.

'May the devil take you!' the retort came back from inside.

'Stebbins, if you please,' interrupted Ravenscroft, not wanting any delay in his request.

The jailer muttered something under his breath before continuing on his way.

'I shall be glad to get out of this place,' said Crabb.

'Stebbins. Number thirteen,' announced Smith, stopping abruptly outside one of the doors. The jailer placed a key in the lock and opened the door.

As the detectives entered the gloomy, airless room, a shadowy figure that had been lying on a straw mattress rose quickly from its resting place.

'Lord bless you, Inspector Ravenscroft, I knew you would come!' exclaimed the youth.

'Stebbins,' replied Ravenscroft.

'Lord, if it is not Constable Crabb as well.'

'Sergeant, now,' corrected the younger policeman.

'Well, Stebbins, you seem to have got yourself into a bad situation this time,' said Ravenscroft.

'I didn't do it, Inspector Ravenscroft.'

'Thank you, Smith, you can leave us now. We wish to be alone with the prisoner, if you please. We will knock on the door when we need you.'

The jailer gave Ravenscroft a cold stare and muttered something inaudible as he began to make his way out of the cell.

'And I would be obliged if you could leave the lantern with us,' instructed Ravenscroft.

Smith placed the lamp on the small table, before banging the door loudly behind him.

'I knew that my Maisie would contact you,' said Stebbins excitedly. 'I always said to her that if anything was to happen to one of us, the other was to let you know. Inspector Ravenscroft will always see us right, I said.'

'They say you killed your uncle?' asked Ravenscroft.

'But I didn't do it. You has to believe me.'

'Let us begin at the beginning,' said Ravenscroft thoughtfully. 'Where did your uncle reside?'

'Bromsgrove. He had a little shop in one of the courts there. He sold anti— anti— old books, and things like that.'

'Were you in the habit of visiting your uncle?'

'Not very often. I had not seen him for years until two weeks ago.'

'But you visited him recently? Why was that?'

'Me and Maisie wants to get on in the world. We wants to start our own little business. This nice little property has just come up in Pershore. We thought we could buy it and start our own boarding establishment. There is room for five or six paying guests. Maisie could do the cooking and I would do everything else. We has a few pounds put by, but not enough to buy it outright.'

'So you thought your uncle might lend you the money?'

'Yes, but Uncle Stebby, he said no. He made it a rule never to lend to relations, he said. He was always a bit tight, was Uncle Stebby.'

'So you came away empty-handed. What happened next? I am sorry to ask you all these questions, Stebbins, but if Sergeant Crabb and I are to be of any help to you, it is important that we know as much as we can,' said Ravenscroft.

'Maisie, she says I was to go back to my uncle and ask again. I knew that he would never lend us the money, but I didn't like to disappoint my Maisie.'

'So you went back to the shop?'

'Yes.'

'When was that?'

'A week ago.'

'What time did you arrive?'

'It was about half past five in the afternoon, I think. It was dark and foggy, you couldn't see your nose in front of your face, it was so murky.'

'When you arrived at your uncle's premises did you see anyone entering or leaving the shop?'

'No, I don't think so.'

'Did you notice anyone looking in the shop window, or anyone loitering about in the vicinity?' Ravenscroft paced the floor of the narrow cell as he spoke.

'No.'

'Please, go on with your narrative.'

'Well I pushes open the door. As there was no one in the shop I called out, but no one answered.'

'And what happened next?'

'So I went into the room at the back of the shop. I knew Uncle Stebby sometimes worked at his desk there, and that he was a bit hard of hearing. It was terrible, Inspector Ravenscroft. There was blood everywhere, all over the floor,' replied Stebbins, becoming more and more agitated.

'Was there anyone else in the room?'

'No, only my uncle, he was slumped across his desk. I went up to him. There was this big knife in his back. God's honour, Inspector, it weren't me that did it.'

Ravenscroft placed a comforting hand on the youth's shoulder. 'What happened next?' he asked gently.

'Next thing was I heard the shop door opening and this man's voice calls out for my uncle. God help me, I didn't know what to do, Inspector, but I never did it,' sobbed Stebbins.

'Control yourself, Stebbins. What did this man do?'

'He comes into the back room and sees me standing there, at the back of the desk, with all that blood. Then he rushes back into the main room and then outside calling, "Murder! Murder! Help!" Lord help me, but I didn't know what to do. I couldn't move. The next thing I knows is this policeman runs into the shop, and he takes one look at me and says, "Now then, lad, back away from the body." Then he puts the cuffs on me.'

'Can you describe the man who came into the shop?'

'He was a gentleman. He was well dressed, about forty I would think, a bit taller than you, but not as tall as Sergeant Crabb.'

'I don't suppose he gave his name?'

'No.'

'So they took you to the local police station in Bromsgrove? Do you remember who questioned you there?'

'Big bully of a man, said his name was Bull something or other,' replied a distraught Stebbins.

'Bullman?'

'Yes, that's it. Bullman. Do you know him, Inspector Ravenscroft?'

'Yes, Detective Inspector Stanley Bullman of the Bromsgrove Constabulary. I have never met the said gentleman, but I know of his somewhat awesome reputation.'

'They put me in a cell and questioned me for nearly two days. This Bullman, he shouts at me all the time. He kept saying to me that if I confessed to the crime things would go easy for me.'

'And did you confess?'

'No. I told him I didn't do it, but Bullman would not listen. Finally he charges me with the murder, and then they sent me here to this horrible prison in Worcester. He said that I would be put on trial for what I had done, and that I would hang. You is the first person I have seen in three days. Thank God my Maisie contacted you. Honestly, as my mother's name was Mary, I never did this terrible thing. You has to believe me. I don't want to hang!' implored Stebbins. 'You knows that I am innocent. I would never do a thing like that.'

'Rest assured, Stebbins, that we will do all that we can to help you. Crabb, if you will, please summon the jailer.'

'Yes, sir.' Crabb banged on the door.

'How long is it since you had a decent meal?' asked Ravenscroft.

'Last proper meal I had was with my Maisie before I set off to see poor Uncle Stebby. They only give me bread and water in here.'

'Ah, Mr Smith,' Ravenscroft addressed the jailer as he entered the cell. 'Here is a shilling. I would be obliged if you would send out for a dinner and a tankard of best ale from one of the nearby inns for this prisoner.'

'Can't do that. It's against the rules,' muttered Smith.

'And here is another shilling for your pains,' continued Ravenscroft, ignoring the last remark and placing both coins in the jailer's hand. 'When I next return here, if I find that my wishes have been satisfactory carried out, then I will give you another shilling, and put in a good word for you with your superiors. Should I find, however, that you have neglected my instructions, or that you have treated the prisoner in a shameful way, then I will ensure that things will go badly for you. I trust you understand my meaning?'

'Yes, sir,' replied Smith, giving a slight nod of his head.

'Excellent. Well, Stebbins, have courage. Sergeant Crabb and I will see what is to be done.'

'God bless you, Inspector Ravenscroft. I knew that you would never let me down.'

Ravenscroft gave a brief smile of encouragement as he left the cell.

'Bless you, sir,' called out Stebbins, as the door closed to with a bang.

CHAPTER TWO

BROMSGROVE

'Have you never met with this Inspector Bullman, sir?' asked Crabb. The two policemen had arrived at the police station, in the Worcestershire market town of Bromsgrove, and Crabb had quickly secured the services of a passing constable to see to their horse and trap.

'No, I have never had that pleasure, but I certainly know of his reputation,' replied Ravenscroft.

'You sound as though you do not entirely approve of him?'

'Bullman is known as a tough man. He has a good record for arresting criminals and securing convictions, but from what I have heard he does not always follow the correct procedure. I have a feeling that we will have to tread carefully.' Ravenscroft opened the door of the police station.

'Good morning. How can I help you?' asked a fresh-faced uniformed officer standing behind the counter.

'Good morning to you, Constable. I am Detective Inspector Ravenscroft, and this is my colleague, Detective Sergeant Crabb. We are both from Ledbury, and we would like to speak with Detective Inspector Bullman. I would be obliged if you could inform him of our arrival.'

'Yes, Inspector,' replied the officer standing quickly to attention. 'If you will give me one minute, I will see if Inspector Bullman is able to see you.'

'Nice station,' remarked Crabb as the two men waited.

'I believe that they have recently undertaken some improvements.'

The officer soon returned to the room and led them into a large hallway, where he knocked on one of the doors.

'Come in!' shouted a loud voice.

The two detectives entered the room, where they found a short squat detective, with ruffled hair and an unshaven red face, dressed in an old tweed suit, a plain shirt and a stained canary-coloured waistcoat, who was sitting behind a desk littered with untidy piles of paper.

Ravenscroft cleared his throat. 'I take it I have the honour of addressing Detective Inspector Bullman of the Bromsgrove Constabulary?'

'You do — and you are Riverswood from . . . ?' began Bullman.

'Detective Inspector Ravenscroft from Ledbury Police Station, and this is Detective Sergeant Crabb.'

'Ah yes, Ravenscroft. I've heard of you.' Bullman placed some tobacco in his mouth and chewed vigorously. 'What brings you here? It's a long way from your domain.'

'We have been asked to make further enquiries regarding a certain youth who goes by the name of Stebbins.' Ravenscroft chose his words carefully.

'Guilty! He murdered his uncle in cold blood. He wanted the old man's money for some dubious business venture. Caught red-handed, he was. You won't find him here though,' replied Bullman.

'No, we have just visited him in Worcester Jail,' said Ravenscroft, sensing that the policeman was adopting a defensive manner, and that he and Crabb were being eyed with a degree of suspicion.

'Then you know that he is to stand trial, and that he will almost certainly hang.'

'Pardon me for asking, but how can you be so certain that he is guilty?'

'Because I have been a policeman for over thirty years, and I know a guilty man when I see one. Besides he was caught, all covered in blood, with his hand on the blade. What more do you want?' replied Bullman in what Ravenscroft regarded as an almost confrontational tone of voice.

Ravenscroft looked at Crabb.

'I suppose you didn't know that, did you? Well, I have a witness who saw him. Now if you will excuse me, I have to get on.'

'I am sure you are correct, but I have to inform you that we have been requested to make further enquiries into this case.'

'Damn it!' Bullman brought his fist down on to the table with such violence that a pile of papers slid of the desk and on to the floor. 'Who the devil has asked you to question my judgement?'

'I am afraid I am not at liberty to tell you who has instructed us in this matter. We have been sworn to secrecy.'

'This is insufferable!' snarled Bullman. 'I suppose it's that damned Superintendent in Worcester. He is always interfering in our affairs, sending us letters, telling us what we should, and should not do. Why he cannot leave us alone I don't know. It is not to be countenanced, Ravenscroft, I tell you.'

'I'm sorry but I am not at liberty to say who has authorised us in this matter. Quite honestly Bullman, I have no desire to be here at all. I would much rather be at home in Ledbury, sitting before an open fire with a glass of punch in my hand, at this time of the year, but I have to compile this wretched report into the case.' Ravenscroft forced a smile as Crabb retrieved the fallen papers.

'Confound it!' snapped Bullman. 'This will not do, Ravenscroft.'

'I know; I too have had to suffer similar annoyances and interferences from superior officers in the past. It is an intolerable situation, but if you could tell us all you know about the case, then Sergeant Crabb and I will be on our way. Would it be possible to see where the crime was committed?'

'Constable Roberts here arrested the culprit.' Bullman indicated the policeman who had shown them into the room, and who had been standing silently in the doorway. 'I suppose it will do no harm.'

'Thank you, Inspector. What can you tell us about this witness to the crime?' asked Ravenscroft, pressing home his advantage.

'He is a local gentleman by the name of Nightingale. He lives with his sister in a house at the bottom of New Road. Roberts can take you there if you like. Now if you will excuse me, there is work to be done.'

'Of course.'

'And, Ravenscroft, I would regard it as a courtesy if you would keep me informed of your activities.'

'That goes without saying,' replied Ravenscroft.

The inspector waved his hand in a sign of dismissal before the three policemen left the room.

* * *

A few minutes later, Ravenscroft and Crabb looked up at the fine town house in New Road.

'Constable Roberts, before we interview Mr Nightingale, I wonder whether you could tell us what took place on the day of the crime?' asked Ravenscroft.

'I was on patrol in the area, when suddenly I heard a voice crying out, "Murder! Murder! Help!" I raced along the passageway towards the shop, where I saw the witness standing outside in a most agitated manner.'

'There was quite a fog at this time I believe?'

'Yes, sir. It was with some difficulty that I was able to see the gentleman.'

'Tell me Roberts, did you see anyone running away from the shop premises?'

'No, sir.'

'Was there anyone else in the vicinity?'

'I don't think so.'

'Go on with your account, if you would,' urged Ravenscroft.

'I ran up to the gentleman, who informed me that a terrible murder had just taken place inside the premises. I then proceeded cautiously into the shop, and then into the smaller room at the back where I saw the youth, Stebbins, standing over the body of the dead man.'

'I am sorry to interrupt you, Roberts, but can you tell us whether the body was on the floor or in the chair?'

'The bookseller was slumped over the desk. There was a knife in his back. There was blood everywhere, over the desk and on the floor. I later discovered that he had been stabbed three or four times in a terrible manner.'

'It certainly sounds like a frenzied attack,' added Ravenscroft.

'The lad, Stebbins, looked terrified. As he was standing at the back of the desk behind the victim, I put the handcuffs on him. I then summoned further assistance. Inspector Bullman arrived shortly afterwards and took away the suspect for further questioning. I then took a statement from the witness, Mr Nightingale.'

'It seems as though you have been most thorough. How long have you been with the force?'

'Nearly six months.'

'Do you like your work?'

'Yes, sir. It is most interesting,' smiled the young policeman.

'Good. Oh, just one more question. You said just now that Detective Inspector Bullman arrived on the scene quite quickly. How long was it before he arrived?'

'About two or three minutes, I believe.'

'That seems quite soon.'

'When I summoned assistance with my whistle it was answered by my colleague, Constable Masters. He ran back to the station and returned with the inspector.'

Having ascertained all he could from Roberts, Ravenscroft rang the bell. After a few seconds, the door was opened by a plain, middle-aged woman.

'Good afternoon. My name is Detective Inspector Ravenscroft. I understand that this is the residence of Mr Nightingale.'

'It is. Peter Nightingale is my brother,' answered the woman giving the detective a cautious look.

'I would be grateful if my colleague and I could have a few moments of his time. It is about the murder that he recently witnessed.'

'You had better come in.'

As they stepped into the hallway, Ravenscroft observed that the woman's face was lined, that she moved in a slow, careful and almost painful manner, and that her black hair was parted in the middle in the old-fashioned way.

'If you would care to wait here, I will see if my brother is free to see you. He is a busy man, as I am sure you will appreciate.'

'Of course, I understand.'

The woman tapped lightly on one of the doors that led off the hall.

'Come in, Mary.'

'There are some policemen here to see you, Peter. They want to question you further regarding that terrible murder.'

'I have provided a statement to the police. I do not know what I can possibly add to what I have said already,' said a tall, middle-aged man, rising from a chair behind a large mahogany desk.

'Forgive the intrusion, sir. My name is Detective Inspector Ravenscroft. This is Detective Sergeant Crabb, and I think you know Constable Roberts. I have been asked to make further enquiries concerning this case.'

'I cannot see why. It was a terrible business, and I have no great desire to dwell on it more than I have to.'

'It is procedure. Sometimes it is necessary to clarify certain points of evidence before the trial commences. I can assure you that we will not take up too much of your time.' Ravenscroft removed his hat with a smile.

'Well, if you insist. You had better take a seat.'

Ravenscroft looked around the comfortably furnished, book-lined room, and wondered whether it had been Nightingale himself who had arranged it in such an elegant way, or whether the neat interior owed more to his sister's hand.

'Perhaps you and your colleagues would like some tea, Inspector?' asked Mary Nightingale.

'That is most kind, but that will not be necessary,' replied Ravenscroft accepting the seat, as Crabb and Roberts stood by the door.

'Thank you, Mary. You can leave us now,' said Nightingale.

Ravenscroft thought he detected a slight hesitation in her manner. Mary Nightingale looked at her brother intently before she left the room.

'Now, Inspector, what else do you need to know?' Peter Nightingale resumed his seat behind the desk. He adjusted his spectacles as he stared at the detectives.

'I would be grateful if you would describe what took place at the bookshop on the day of the murder,' said Ravenscroft.

'Certainly.' Nightingale spoke in a deliberate and detailed manner. 'I entered the bookshop. There was no one there, so I called out for the proprietor. Receiving no answer, I walked up the two steps to the back room at the rear of the shop, where I found a youth standing over poor Mr Stebbins. There was blood everywhere and I could see the bookseller had been stabbed in the back. It was clear that the crime had just been committed by the youth. I decided to summon help and walked quickly to the outer door, where I shouted that a murder had been perpetrated. Fortunately Constable Roberts was in the vicinity, so I did not have long to wait. When Roberts arrived, I explained what I had just witnessed. We both re-entered the premises, where we confronted the murderer. Roberts arrested him, further assistance was called for, the youth was taken away, and I made my way to the police station where I gave my statement. That is all there is to relate.'

'You say that it was clear that the crime had been committed by the youth,' said Ravenscroft as Crabb made notes in his pocketbook. 'Why were you so sure of this? It could have been that Stebbins had entered the shop momentarily before yourself, and had discovered the body.'

'I do not think that was the case.'

'But you did not actually see Stebbins stab the book seller?'

'No, but when he saw me a look of terror came over his face, as though he was surprised to have been caught in the act.'

'Inspector Bullman has told us that you saw Stebbins with his hand on the knife?'

'That is not quite right. He was certainly standing over the dead man.'

'But you did not see his hand on the knife?'

'No, I suppose not.'

'I believe the weather was quite bad at the time. When you approached the bookshop were you aware of anyone else either in the area, or coming out of the premises?'

'No, I don't think so.'

'Do you think there was anyone else other than Stebbins, in the shop, or that someone could have been hiding there?'

'No.'

'You are sure on that point? Someone who could have slipped past you?'

'I do not think so.'

'May I ask the reason for your visit to the bookshop that day?'

'Certainly. As you can see I am a collector of fine books, mainly first editions, and in particular those written by Mr Anthony Trollope. My library includes all of his works, although the last novel in the Barsetshire series, *The Last Chronicle of Barset*, has always eluded me. I had asked old Stebbins to inform me when he had acquired the work. You are familiar with the works of Trollope, Inspector Ravenscroft?'

'My wife has read a number of his books, but I have not.'

'Then that pleasure still awaits you.' Nightingale returned Ravenscroft's smile. 'On the morning in question, I had received a letter from Stebbins, informing me that he had been successful in obtaining a copy of the elusive work. That was the reason for my visit.'

'Do you still have this letter?'

'No.'

'Oh? Why is that?' asked Ravenscroft, sensing that for the first time in their interview the other's calm, methodical exterior had been disturbed.

'I destroyed the letter, along with some other papers of mine yesterday morning. I do not like to keep unwanted items of correspondence.'

'That is a pity.'

'I do not understand the reason for all these questions, Inspector. I don't particularly care for your tone of voice. I feel I am being almost treated like a suspect. I think you should leave.' Nightingale rose abruptly from his chair.

'You are certainly not a suspect in this case, Mr Nightingale. It is just that we need to know the reason for your visit, that is all,' replied Ravenscroft hastily, realising that perhaps he had gone too far in his questioning. 'No offence was intended.'

'There was none taken.' Nightingale had already regained his composure. He resumed his seat.

'You have known Mr Stebbins for many years?' said Ravenscroft, quickly changing the subject.

'Since my sister and I moved to Bromsgrove, some fifteen years ago, after the demise of our late father.'

'What was Mr Stebbins like, as a person?'

'He was very reserved. He spoke very little. He was not one to suffer fools gladly, and he usually drove a hard bargain. I would say that he was very difficult to know. He often seemed to be in a bad temper, and it was often difficult to engage him in conversation.'

'And Mr Stebbins has supplied you with many books over the years?'

‘Indeed. I would say that nearly half the books that you see in this room were supplied by Stebbins. My sister, Mary, says we will have to move house again should I continue to add to my collection,’ said Nightingale, almost in a light-hearted way.

‘I can see that you are a gentleman of means,’ said Ravenscroft.

‘Would it were so. Although we were left annuities by my father, we find it is not adequate to provide for all of life’s domestic luxuries. My sister is also not in the best of health.’

‘I am sorry to hear that.’

‘Unfortunately she has a serious medical condition, for which there is no cure. The symptoms can be relieved, but her treatment is quite costly and does necessitate funding. So I am afraid that I must supplement my income by other means. I am an insurance agent for The Liverpool, London and Globe Insurance Company.’

‘That must be interesting work.’

‘Far from it; it is quite mundane and ordinary, but necessary, as I have explained.’

‘I presume that you arrange life insurance policies?’

‘Indeed.’

‘Was Mr Stebbins insured by your company?’

‘Alas, he was not one of my clients. I did mention it to him on several occasions, but he always said it was a waste of money in his case, as he had no one who would benefit when his time came. Let us say that Mr Stebbins was a man who protected his own financial interests.’

‘Can you elaborate further?’

‘I suppose you would call him mean. He did not appear to spend much on his appearance. I swear he has worn the same coat and trousers since I have known him. He lived in a frugal fashion in rooms above the shop, I believe.’

‘So you did not mix socially with the said gentleman?’

‘Certainly not. I only ever saw him in the shop. Our relationship was only of a business nature.’

‘Well, Mr Nightingale, you have been most helpful.’ Ravenscroft rose from the chair.

The door suddenly opened.

Ravenscroft concluded that although Mary Nightingale had been excluded from the room by her brother, she had probably heard everything that had transpired.

'I am more than welcome to assist you in the future, in any way I can. I must also apologise for my hasty remarks made earlier,' said Nightingale.

'That is quite alright, sir. Thank you for your co-operation. Miss Nightingale,' said Ravenscroft, before taking his leave of the brother and sister.

* * *

The three policemen made their way in silence down the hill towards the main street of the town, passing by a number of smart-looking houses and a large timber-framed building on their right.

As they neared the corner of the road, they were met by a group of carol singers.

'Could you spare a coin for the poor and destitute of Bromsgrove?' said one of the singers, a tall young man of a cheery disposition, who came forward to greet Ravenscroft.

The detective reached into his pocket.

'Thank you, sir, you will have the satisfaction of knowing that your contribution will go towards providing a Christmas dinner for the inmates of the local workhouse,' smiled the carol singer.

'Then I am pleased for it,' said Ravenscroft. 'Roberts, will you now take us to the shop?'

'A merry Christmas to you all,' shouted the young man as the carol singers resumed their singing.

'A merry Christmas to you as well,' returned Ravenscroft, as Crabb added to the young man's collection.

As Ravenscroft and his two companions made their way along the main street of the town, he looked up at the three- and four-storey buildings on either side of the road. Here the various grocers, bakers, tailors and butchers displayed their wares, either in their windows or outside their premises. A small boy was gazing longingly at the display in the window of The Home and Colonial Stores, and one or two horse-drawn vehicles made their way along the imposing thoroughfare.

After a few yards, Roberts turned off the High Street, and the three men were soon walking along a narrow cobbled alleyway, across which a number of old half-timbered buildings stood facing one another.

'Good grief!' exclaimed Ravenscroft, tripping over what looked like a bundle of rags near one of the doorways.

'Penny for Christmas,' said a voice.

'I am sorry I did not see you there,' said Ravenscroft, recovering from his stumble.

'Penny for Christmas,' repeated the croaky voice.

Ravenscroft looked down at the old ragged man, who rattled a tin mug in his direction.

'Spare a penny for a poor destitute fellow, who has no home to go to for Christmas,' pleaded the beggar.

The detective reached into his pocket, and dropped a coin into the tin.

'Lord bless you, governor! St Peter will put in a good word for you on the Day of Judgement.'

'I would certainly hope so; I have done enough good deeds to earn my place,' smiled Ravenscroft. 'I think we should now proceed towards the scene of the crime, Roberts, before my purse is completely emptied by the inhabitants of this town.'

'Move along there, Jonas, before the next gentleman trips over you,' said Roberts, addressing the beggar.

The beggar rose to his feet, muttering under his breath as he did so, and after collecting two parcels covered in old newspaper, began to make his way slowly out of the alleyway.

'Here we are,' said Roberts as the group neared the end of the walkway.

He had brought them to a small timbered building, the bull's-eye windows of which revealed a display of several piles of untidy books. A creaking, cracked sign above the doorway was marked with the words 'Stebbins — Fine Books' in faded antique lettering, and Ravenscroft observed the paint on the outside windowsills was badly chipped and worn.

'We have kept the premises locked since the murder.' Roberts placed a large rusty key in the door. 'Everything should be just as it was left.'

'Thank you, Roberts, but before we enter, I think you may leave us. Sergeant Crabb and I would prefer to look round on our own. I will see that we lock up once we have concluded our business here, and we will also return the key to the station in due course.'

'Yes, sir,' replied the constable, before making his way back down the alley.

'Well, Tom, let us see what we can discover inside.' Ravenscroft turned the key and pushed open the creaking oak door.

As the two detectives entered the dimly lit shop they were confronted by a smell of damp and old leather.

'He certainly had plenty of stock,' remarked Crabb, looking round at the book-lined room.

'Some of it looks as if it has been here for generations.' Ravenscroft picked up a book from one of the piles that were stacked at various intervals on the floor. He blew the dust into the air where it seemed to linger in the half-light, before settling gently on to other volumes.

'I've never seen so many books in one place,' said Crabb.

'He must have sold some of them from time to time,' remarked Ravenscroft, looking up at the cobwebs that clung to the corners of the ceiling. 'What a dreary confined place to live out one's existence. That must be the inner room where the old man was killed.'

Ravenscroft and Crabb climbed up the two steps that led into a smaller room at the back of the shop.

'This is where he sat, at this desk. From here he would have had a good view of all the customers who entered his shop,' said Ravenscroft. 'As he was stabbed in the back, I think we can safely conclude that he must have known his killer, to have allowed him into his inner sanctum and let him come behind him while he was seated.'

'Bloodstains.' Crabb pointed to the floor.

'Yes; and there are stains also on the chair and desk. It was a savage attack, but why? One blow would surely have killed him; there was no need for all of this.'

'Whoever committed the crime must have hated the old man a great deal.'

'Indeed. If we are to believe Stebbins, and I have no reason to doubt his testimony, when he entered the room he said his uncle was already dead and the floor was still wet with blood. This would suggest that the crime must have taken place some minutes before young Stebbins arrived. The killer must have already made good his escape, no doubt slipping unnoticed into the fog. There was nowhere here, as far as I can see, that the killer could have secreted himself from view, when Stebbins, and then Nightingale and Roberts entered the shop.'

'Bullman said that Nightingale told him that Stebbins was standing over the dead man, his hand on the knife,' interjected Crabb.

'Yes, that was why I was anxious to question Nightingale on that point. Stebbins was obviously shaken by what he had just discovered; it was his misfortune that Nightingale entered the shop at that moment. When we questioned Nightingale he admitted that Stebbins did not have his hand actually on the knife, but Bullman seemed more than enthusiastic to believe that Nightingale had told him otherwise. I wonder why?'

'You said that Inspector Bullman has a good record for catching criminals?'

'That is so,' said Ravenscroft. 'Was Bullman anxious for Stebbins to confess to the crime so that he could bring the case to a satisfactory conclusion? Or does he know something more about this case than he cares to admit?'

'What did you make of Nightingale?'

'He is certainly of interest to me. He appears to be living quite comfortably in what must be one of the most elegant houses in Bromsgrove, and yet he undertakes work as an insurance agent to supplement his income and to pay for his sister's medical bills. On the outside he seemed very calm and orderly, but did you notice how quickly he became annoyed when I questioned him about the letter that he had received from the bookseller. Then, just as quickly, he recovered his composure and continued as though nothing had happened. Then there is the sister. Clearly she is not well, but I feel that she has a great influence over her brother. She was very annoyed with him when he asked her to leave, and her quick return to the room at the conclusion of our interview suggested that she had been listening intently on the other side of the door.'

'Do you believe that story he gave us about the letter and the book?'

'I don't know, Tom. I suppose he may have been telling us the truth.'

'Could he be our killer?'

'Our murderer would have been covered in blood after the attack; it would have been difficult for him to walk the streets of Bromsgrove unremarked. However it was a dark, foggy evening, and our killer may have removed his cloak before the attack, then replaced it afterwards, which would have covered any bloodstains on his clothes. Nightingale's house is not five minutes from here. If he was our killer, he could have returned home, changed his clothes, and then quickly returned to the shop, where he waited for someone else to enter the premises so that he could implicate them in the murder. However that perhaps does not make sense. If you or I had just killed someone, why would we then return to the scene of the crime a few minutes later? Surely we would have been unwilling to do that, leaving it for someone else to discover the body and call the police?'

'I suppose you are correct.'

'But then again, perhaps if either you or I had just committed a crime, especially one as brutal as this one, would we have been thinking in a straightforward manner? Criminals do not always act in a calm methodical way, especially when they have committed a crime like this one. Now looking around this room, Tom, what do you notice?'

'Nothing seems disturbed.'

'Exactly. There are no signs of either a struggle, or of anyone conducting a frantic search for goods of value. The books all appear to be in their place; there is nothing on the floor. I wonder what is in the drawer of the desk?' said Ravenscroft. 'See here, a tray containing quite a large number of copper, silver and gold coins. There must be several pounds here.'

'So robbery cannot have been the reason for the attack.'

'Unless there were also notes here, but if that had been the case, I am sure our attacker would have taken the gold sovereigns as well. No, I think we can conclude that Mr Stebbins did not die at the hands of a burglar.'

'But the killer could have taken some valuable antiquarian book?'

'We cannot rule it out, of course — but would not the dust on these old books be disturbed, if somebody had conducted a search for a valuable tome? No, I believe our killer did not know the value of the books.'

'So if old Mr Stebbins was not murdered for his money, or for one of his books, then why was he killed?' asked Crabb, bewildered.

'That is what we have to find out,' replied Ravenscroft, looking around him. 'This is rather strange, Tom. Do you notice something odd about this room?'

'Odd, sir?'

'Yes. There is no further door, and yet I fancy the old man lived above the premises.'

'There could be a door to his rooms leading directly off the alleyway?' suggested Crabb.

'I did not observe before we entered the building that there was another entrance. There is, however, some oak panelling over there on that wall, behind the desk, whereas there are bookcases on the left and right sides.' Ravenscroft tapped the woodwork with his knuckles. 'Ah, this sounds hollow. Now, if I give it a gentle push, will it yield? Yes — we have success!'

'Good Lord!' exclaimed Crabb gazing at the flight of steps that had now been revealed.

'Follow me, Tom, and keep a look out for any traces of blood on the treads or walls.'

The two men made their way up the narrow winding staircase. They found a sparsely furnished room at the top of the flight.

'What a miserable place,' remarked Crabb looking around at the old wooden table, chair and cracked sink. Another door was in the far wall.

'And this looks like the remains of his last meal on this plate. There is another door over there, which I suppose must lead to his sleeping quarters.'

'No signs of any bloodstains.'

'No. I don't think our murderer left from here. There is only one small window, and that is not large enough for a man to squeeze through.' Ravenscroft opened the door to the inner room. Like the first room, it had little furniture: an old bed, a wardrobe and a dressing table.

'This room is little less sad-looking.'

'You are right, Tom. But whatever is that foul smell?' Ravenscroft brought his handkerchief quickly to his nose.

'The old man's night soil,' answered Crabb, giving a swift glance at the chamber pot by his feet.

'Take a look in that wardrobe, while I see if there is anything of note in these drawers,' said Ravenscroft. 'Let us be as quick as we can. I have no desire to linger here longer than is necessary.'

The two met set to work.

'Nothing; only clothes, mostly of an old-fashioned and well-worn nature,' said Ravenscroft, after a few seconds had elapsed. 'Old Mr Stebbins seems to have lived a rather reclusive, parsimonious existence.'

'Again, there is only a very small window, which looks out on to the street.'

'If our murderer hid up here when he heard Stebbins enter the shop, then he certainly could not have left from here after everyone had gone, for the windows are too small and the building was secured — and there are no signs of any blood stains on the floor or furniture. No, I think our killer had already fled before Stebbins arrived. There is also no indication of a frantic search here for anything which the old man might have concealed. If there is an answer for this crime, it must be downstairs.'

The two detectives made their way down the winding, creaking staircase, closing the panelled entrance behind them.

'There must be something else here that can help us. What's this book?' Ravenscroft reached out for a large closed volume that lay on the desk. 'A ledger of some sort, I would say. Yes, see here, Tom, it is a record of the sales he made each day.'

'He does not appear to have been very busy. Two or three books a day.'

'Yes, and on some days there would appear to be no sales at all. *North and South*, three volumes priced at two shillings; Tennyson's *Poems* at threepence; Mrs Beeton's *Book of Household Management*, one shilling,' said Ravenscroft, reading out loud. 'And on the other side of each page we have his daily outgoings — twopence for new candles, sixpence for books purchased, a penny for bread. There is nothing of note here. It all seems rather ordinary. I can't see why anyone would want to kill such a man as this.'

'The crime surely cannot have been committed by any relatives for inheritance. His income seems barely to cover his outgoings.'

'Young Stebbins was surely being optimistic when he asked his uncle for a loan. It seems a lonely life, doesn't it? According to Stebbins, even he did not visit his uncle very often. You cannot but feel sorry for people when they have been reduced to this station in life, but then I suppose it was the life he had chosen, and maybe he was quite happy in his own way. Maybe the books were his companions, and he gained solace from them? I wonder what else there is in this desk.' Ravenscroft reached down and opened the drawer beneath that which had contained the tray of money. 'Just inks, blotting paper and pens here. Let us try the bottom drawer. Nothing; it is quite empty.'

'Why keep a drawer empty?' asked Crabb.

'Wait a moment. It is just as I thought. If I reach into the back, it slides. It is a secret compartment. These desks were often constructed to contain such secretive places where jewellery and other personal items of value could be hidden. Yes, there is something hidden here.'

'It looks just like another book.'

'This one is larger than a pocketbook,' said Ravenscroft, retrieving the bulky volume and placing it upon the desk, before adjusting his spectacles. 'It appears to be well worn. The writing is in the same hand. It seems to be a list of names, with sums of money recorded at the side of each one.'

'The first entry is dated nearly thirty years ago,' added Crabb, looking over Ravenscroft's shoulder at the volume on the desk.

'Many of the sums are quite small, some shillings there, then a few pounds here, the odd guinea or so, but then there are some larger amounts as the years go by. There must be two to three hundred pages of entries. See here, there is one for ten pounds, another for twenty. Then there is another column containing ticks in red and other sums of money recorded. Of course, what we are seeing here is the old man's personal account book, and these sums of money are loans, with the end column showing how much has been repaid. I think our old gentleman was some kind of moneylender.'

'If he was lending out all this money, he does not appear to have benefited from it,' remarked Crabb.

'I agree with you, Tom. If he was lending out all this money for all these years, and making such a tidy profit for his endeavours, then why was he living such a meagre, miserable existence?'

'"Miser" is a word that comes to mind, sir.'

'That is the most likely answer. The bookshop was merely an excuse for his moneylending activities, and as he acquired more and more money from the repaid loans over the years, so he became more and more loath to part with any of his gains, and he certainly did not spend any of it upon himself.'

'So maybe he kept some of that money on the premises?'

'Or he hid it somewhere else. Either way, I think we may have stumbled on the reason for his murder. There must be a strong possibility that one of his creditors committed the crime, either to secure the money, or to seek revenge for some wrong that the old moneylender had previously inflicted upon him. If we study this book carefully there may be some way to finding out who killed Mr Stebbins. Most of the entries at the beginning of the book also have a red tick by their side, showing that the debt has long been repaid. It looks as though he charged quite high rates of interest, even for those times. Let's turn towards the end and see which loans were outstanding at the time of his death.' Ravenscroft pointed to one name on the last completed page. 'See there, Tom?'

'Nightingale!' exclaimed Crabb.

'Yes, ten pounds loaned three months ago, and not repaid. There again is his name on the previous page, for last year, sum of five pounds but that one seems to have been repaid. So our Mr Nightingale is not as affluent as he makes out.'

'You think he committed the crime to avoid having to repay his debt?' asked Crabb.

'That is a possibility, although ten pounds is a comparatively small sum.'

'Men have killed for less.'

'That is true, but I do not think we should jump to any conclusions at this stage in our investigations. Good heavens,

Bullman's name also appears here! He was loaned the sum of five pounds two months ago.'

'So Inspector Bullman knew the murdered man.'

'There must be others listed here who owed larger sums. Yes, see there. Sir John Critchwood, loaned the sum of two hundred and fifty pounds, three months ago, and unpaid at the time of the old miser's death.'

'A great deal of money,' commented Crabb.

'It is indeed, and looking at these other entries, I would say that it is by far the greatest sum recorded here. None of the other debtors owed more than twenty pounds.'

'Who is this Sir John Critchwood?'

'The name is unfamiliar to me. Perhaps a local landowner of some description. See if you can find a recent copy of the Post Office Directory for Worcestershire, or for any of the surrounding counties, on one of the shelves. If you take the main room, I will go through these shelves in this room,' instructed Ravenscroft, beginning to run his finger along the lines of books.

'Yes, sir.'

'It seems that our friend was possessed of a methodical turn of mind. The books all seem perfectly arranged, by subject and then author,' said Ravenscroft.

'The same here,' shouted Crabb from the other room.

'Ah, here we are!' exclaimed Ravenscroft. He took down a large, red-fronted book from one of the shelves. 'Post Office Directory for Worcestershire; it is two years old, but it may suffice. Court Section. Yes, here we are. Sir John Critchwood, Old Dodford Manor, Bournheath.'

'I know where Bournheath is,' said Crabb. 'It's a small village two or three miles north of Bromsgrove.'

'Excellent. What time is it, Tom?'

'It is just past two o'clock.'

'Then I think we should have time to call upon the said gentleman before nightfall. We have done all we can here today. Lock up the premises behind us if you will, Tom.'

Ravenscroft and Crabb made their way out of the shop.

'I must say it is a relief to go back into the fresh air, after all that damp decay and those musty old books, even if the temperature is rather cold.' Ravenscroft buttoned up his coat and drew his scarf close around his neck. 'I notice that the alleyway has no other way out, other than the way we came. The bookshop is nearly at the end. I wonder what that shop is opposite? Its occupant must have a good view of Mr Stebbins' premises.'

The two men crossed over to the timber-framed building, above the door of which was written 'Mrs Alice Marquis, Seamstress and Dressmaker.'

'I think we should pay the lady a visit. She may prove to be a valuable witness.'

Ravenscroft pushed open the narrow door and a bell chimed as he did so. Crabb followed him into the shop.

An elderly woman was sitting in a wooden chair at the back of the room, which was lined with shelves containing a number of large cardboard boxes. An undressed mannequin stood in one corner, and a dress was draped over a small counter.

'Mrs Marquis, I presume?' enquired Ravenscroft, removing his hat.

'Yes, my dear, how can I be of assistance?' The woman laid aside her needle and thread as she rose slowly to her feet.

'My name is Inspector Ravenscroft, and this is my colleague, Sergeant Crabb. We are making enquiries into the death of Mr Stebbins, the bookseller.'

'A terrible business.' The woman shook her head.

'It is, indeed, a terrible business,' echoed Ravenscroft. 'Do you remember the day when the gentleman was killed?'

'Indeed I do.' She peered at the two policemen through her spectacles. 'All that commotion and that man shouting "murder," and then the policeman coming and taking that young man away. I don't think I will forget that day in a hurry.'

'So you must have a good view from here.' Ravenscroft looked out of the window. 'You must have seen all that took place?'

The woman sighed but said nothing.

'I wonder if you could recall what happened shortly before the murder occurred. Did you see anyone enter the shop?' asked Ravenscroft hopefully.

'I saw no one.'

'Oh,' said Ravenscroft, disappointed.

'It is my eyes, sir, they are quite gone, what with all the sewing I've done over the years. The strain has weakened them. I can scarcely see you, let alone see out of the shop.'

'I am sorry for it,' sympathised Ravenscroft. 'Perhaps Mr Marquis saw something?'

'He is no longer with us. He passed away nearly two years ago.'

'Oh, I am sorry. I hope you will excuse the intrusion.'

'It is no intrusion. Not many people come here now. I can assure you that it is pleasant to have someone new to talk to,' smiled Mrs Marquis.

'Did the local police make enquiries at the time?' asked Ravenscroft.

'No,' replied the seamstress shaking her head again, and adopting a mournful face.

'That was remiss of them,' commented Ravenscroft.

'Would you and your friend care to take tea with me?'

'That is very kind of you, Mrs Marquis, but I'm afraid we must decline. We have to travel to Bournheath and then make our way home to Ledbury.'

'You have come a long way. You had best take care on your return — it will snow before nightfall.'

'You may well be right. Good afternoon to you, Mrs Marquis. Oh, just one more thing. You said just now that you saw the policeman arrive and take the young man away. How do you know he was young, if you could not see across to the shop?' asked Ravenscroft about to make his departure.

'I may not see as well now as I used to, but there is nothing wrong with my hearing. I recognised Constable Roberts's step — he often patrols the alley, and calls in upon me from time to time.'

'That is considerate.'

'He is such a nice young man. He has only been a constable for a few months, I believe.'

'That is so.'

'I could tell it was a young man they were taking away from his voice. He kept calling out that he had not committed the crime.'

'I see,' smiled Ravenscroft.

'I also heard those boots on the cobbles earlier in the afternoon.'

'Boots?' enquired Ravenscroft.

'Yes they were heavy boots; the soles must have been quite thick by the sound that they made.'

'How long was this before the murder?'

'About thirty minutes before. I distinctly heard the sound of those boots coming along the alleyway, and then the opening of the door into Stebbins's shop. Then about five minutes later I heard the door being closed and the sound of the boots on the cobbles again, as he went away, only this time they were different.'

'Different?'

'It sounded as though their owner was in a hurry.'

'I don't suppose you saw what this gentleman looked like?'

'I am sorry.'

'Thank you, Mrs Marquis. I wish you good day.'

* * *

Thirty minutes later the trap entered the small North Worcestershire village of Bournheath, and after asking for directions from a passing farm worker, Ravenscroft and Crabb found themselves travelling up a long driveway towards a large fine Georgian-style building. As they looked across the landscaped grounds, Ravenscroft observed an old chapel in the distance, and a wood sloping down towards some far off hills.

Pulling up the horse outside the main entrance Ravenscroft dismounted and pulled vigorously on the bell-pull at the side of the door, as Crabb gave the horse into the care of a stable lad who ran up at their arrival.

A grey-haired footman opened the door. 'Good afternoon. If you have come for the meeting, I am afraid that Sir John and the others have already started.'

'No. I have not come for the meeting, but I would very much appreciate it if you could inform Sir John of my arrival and say that I would like to speak with him, if you please,' said Ravenscroft.

'Who is that, Travers?' a voice called out from inside the hallway.

'There are two gentlemen here to see Sir John.'

'Meeting is already underway,' said a thick-set man dressed in tweeds, coming forward. 'If you are not expected, you will have to come back another day.'

'Forgive the intrusion, but my name is Detective Inspector Ravenscroft, and this is my colleague, Detective Sergeant Crabb,' began Ravenscroft.

'You are not from the local constabulary,' sniffed the man.

'No. We are making enquiries of a serious nature, and believe that Sir John Critchwood may be able to assist us. Who do I have the honour of addressing?'

'March. I am Sir John's land agent.'

'Well, Mr March, as I said, it is imperative that I speak with Sir John,' Ravenscroft persisted.

'That will not be possible. Sir John is chairing a most important meeting at the present, and cannot be disturbed,' replied March curtly.

'Then perhaps we could wait inside? We have come rather a long way. Do you know how long Sir John will be?'

'Sir John will be busy for the rest of the day. I am afraid I cannot tell you how long the meeting will last for.'

'If you would allow us to enter, perhaps you would give my card to Sir John, so that when the opportunity arises he would be able to have a few words with us. I can assure you that we will not detain Sir John for longer than is necessary,' said Ravenscroft, trying to sound both amiable and firm at the same time.

March studied the two policemen with a sullen, disparaging look.

'It really is of the utmost importance, I can assure you.'

'I suppose you had better come in then.' March waved them in. 'Take a seat there.'

'Thank you, Mr March,' said Ravenscroft. He handed his card to the agent.

March opened a door to the left of the hall, and as he did so the detectives could hear the sound of laughter from within the room.

'Must be an important meeting,' whispered Crabb, as March entered the room and closed the door behind him.

'Yes, we must hope that Sir John is able to spare the time to see us,' replied Ravenscroft.

'Nice place.' Crabb looked around at the fine paintings and furniture that adorned the hall.

'Indeed. One wonders why Sir John felt the need to secure a loan of two hundred and fifty pounds from old Mr Stebbins, if he can afford to furnish his home in such a manner.'

As the door opened briefly again, to more noise and laughter, Ravenscroft leaned forwards to secure a brief glance of the group of men seated around a large table.

'I have given your card to Sir John,' remarked March returning to the hallway, accompanied by a younger man.

'I'm dreadfully sorry, but I am afraid my father is rather busy at the moment. Gosh, I think I have seen you somewhere before,' said the new arrival.

'You were carol singing in Bromsgrove earlier this morning,' replied Ravenscroft.

'So I was — and you gave me a shilling,' laughed the young man.

'For that Christmas dinner for the inmates of Bromsgrove Workhouse.'

'Yes, and mighty appreciative they will be, I am sure.'

'Sir John Critchwood is your father?'

'I'm afraid so; Christopher Critchwood at your service, Inspector Ravenscroft.'

'Then I am pleased to make your acquaintance again, Mr Critchwood.'

'Look you must think we are rude, but the truth is you have caught us on rather a bad day, as I am sure you appreciate. I don't suppose there is any way you could come back tomorrow, is there?'

'I'm sorry, but our investigations are of a serious nature, and cannot possibly be delayed.'

'That sounds rather life-threatening,' laughed Christopher Critchwood.

'We are investigating the death of Mr Stebbins.'

'Oh, that bookseller. It was rather a nasty business, by all accounts. I read about it in the *Bromsgrove Messenger*, but I thought someone had been arrested for the murder?'

'Further information has come to light since then. That is why we need to speak with your father,' said Ravenscroft, pressing home his case.

'God, you don't think my father did it, do you?' said Critchwood light-heartedly.

'We have not yet reached any conclusions.'

Hearing Ravenscroft's serious tone, Critchwood's smile vanished. 'Well, yes, this all sounds pretty serious, as you said. Lord. I think I had better have a word with my father, after all.'

'I would be deeply obliged, Mr Critchwood.'

'Yes . . . well . . . yes,' said Critchwood in a flustered manner. 'Will see what I can do.'

'Let us hope for some success,' said Ravenscroft to Crabb, as Christopher Critchwood left them again.

After a minute or two had elapsed, a loud voice could be heard from the other side of the door. 'Confound the man! Why cannot it wait? Gentlemen, you will have to excuse me.'

'Something tells me that our presence here today will not be welcomed,' said Ravenscroft.

Suddenly the door was flung open and a tall, grey-haired man, walking with the aid of a stick, strode into the hallway.

'Now what the devil is all this about?' demanded Sir John Critchwood, as he closed the door behind him with a bang.

'My name is Detective Inspector Ravenscr—'

'I know who you are; I've read your card. It says you are from Ledbury,' snapped Sir John.

'That is correct, sir.'

'Then what the deuce are you doing here? We have a perfectly good constabulary in Bromsgrove.'

'Indeed you do, but we have been asked by a higher authority to carry out enquiries,' replied Ravenscroft, feeling somewhat overawed by the knight's overbearing manner.

'Higher authority eh? What higher authority? Well you had better come to the point. You have interrupted a most important meeting.'

'Yes, I appreciate that, but I can assure you that —'

'Yes, yes, get on with it.'

'You may have heard of the death of Mr Stebbins the bookseller in Bromsgrove?'

'I read about it last week. I thought Inspector Bullman had caught the man who had committed the crime; some younger relative of the bookseller, if I remember.'

'Did you know the deceased man?' continued Ravenscroft, seeking to ignore the last remark.

'No, never met the fellow.'

'So you never visited the bookshop?'

'No. I suppose I may have walked by on one or two occasions, but I never felt the need to go inside.'

'Did you ever have any business transactions with the gentleman?'

'I've just said I never met him. Were you listening? Is that all? Can I now return to my meeting?'

'That is rather strange, Sir John, because Mr Stebbins was in the habit of lending money to the people of Bromsgrove. He recorded all his activities in this book,' said Ravenscroft, bringing forth the pocketbook from his coat pocket.

'Well? What is all that to do with me?' growled Sir John.

'The book contains an entry relating to Sir John Critchwood, three months ago, for the loan of two hundred and fifty pounds,' said Ravenscroft, anxious to observe what effect his words would have on the landowner.

'What absolute nonsense! Do I look like a man who would want to borrow two hundred and fifty pounds from a backstreet moneylender?' said Sir John, annoyed.

'So you deny that such a transaction ever took place?'

'Of course I deny it!'

'Then how do you explain the entry?'

'Look here Ravenscroft, Ravenswood, or whatever your name is, I must say that I find your tone damned impertinent.' Sir John's voice rose as he spoke. He shook his walking stick at the detectives.

'Are you aware of anyone acting on your behalf in this matter?' continued Ravenscroft, realising that in all probability the end of the interview was fast approaching.

'I've had enough of all this. I am a gentleman, and when a gentleman tells you the truth you should accept it without question. I think you should leave my house. March! March!'

'Here, Sir John,' said the agent.

Ravenscroft turned. He had not been aware that the land agent had been in the room.

'Show these men out,' instructed Sir John, turning on his heel.

'I thank you for your time,' said Ravenscroft, acknowledging that it would be futile to continue with his questioning.

'Rest assured, Ravenscroft, that I will be contacting your superiors tomorrow to report your contemptible manner and attitude towards me.'

'That is your prerogative, sir.'

Sir John opened the door to the meeting room and disappeared quickly from view.

'This way,' said March in a forthright manner as he held open the front door.

'Good day to you, Mr March.'

The agent said nothing, but continued to watch intently as Ravenscroft and Crabb climbed into the trap.

'Well that was abrupt,' remarked Crabb, as he urged the horse forward.

'Indeed. He was lying to us, I am sure of that — but why? Furthermore, why would a man who lives in a house such as this need to borrow money from a backstreet moneylender? A man of his reputation and standing would surely have borrowed from a bank or other financial institution, and possibly on more advantageous terms.'

'Perhaps his credit was not good?' suggested Crabb.

'You could be right. Who knows? We will need to make further enquiries regarding the affairs of Sir John Critchwood before we return to question him further. The weather looks decidedly unpleasant. I think it will not be long before there is a significant fall of snow, and we will need to make good progress if we are to get over the hills and back to Ledbury before nightfall.'

'Right, sir,' said Crabb cracking the whip.

'I tell you one thing, Tom, I would have liked to have been at that meeting. Who were all those men — and what was their business?'

'They told us no end of times it was an important meeting,' agreed Crabb.

'I did however manage to gain a brief glance into the room when the door opened. There must have been about five or six men, all seated around the table — and one of them was our Peter Nightingale!'

CHAPTER THREE

BROMSGROVE, 23 DECEMBER

'I cannot believe that Sir John Critchwood treated you in such an awful manner,' said Lucy, after breakfast had been concluded, the following morning at the cottage in Ledbury.

'I suppose I did ask him some rather unsettling questions,' replied Ravenscroft. 'Perhaps I should have been more tactful.'

'Yes, but you were only doing your duty, and if Sir John had been a proper gentleman, he would have answered you directly and not been so rude.'

'Never mind; at least our journey to Bromsgrove yesterday was not in vain. Finding that book hidden in the bookseller's desk has told us more about the man and his activities than I originally thought possible. It is highly likely that his murderer was one of the people he loaned money to. What Tom and I have to discover is which one, and why he committed the crime.'

'If it's not the terrible Sir John then it is probably that Mr Nightingale, or his strange sister,' joked Lucy.

'Who knows, my dear, you could be right. You often are.'

'There has been quite a fall of snow in the night. Surely you don't intend taking the trap all that way in this weather?' asked Lucy helping Ravenscroft on with his coat.

'Certainly not. The road beneath the British Camp would be quite treacherous today. I will take the train to Bromsgrove, and have arranged for Tom to join me on the way at Malvern Wells Station. We will take a cab from Bromsgrove Station when we arrive.'

'That sounds for the best, but whatever you do — make sure you are back here before nightfall. Richard will be home today, and tomorrow will be Christmas Eve. I have ordered the goose, ready for Christmas Day.'

'That is excellent, my dear. I can assure you that I will do everything in my power to solve this case today, and secure poor Stebbins's release, or I shall try to put off everything until after Christmas. Be assured that I will return. I have no desire to miss Christmas Eve, nor your famous Christmas dinner, in the excellent company of my wife and children.'

* * *

'If this train goes any slower we will get off and walk,' grumbled Ravenscroft, as he and Crabb looked out at the snowy fields from their carriage window. 'It must be at least half an hour since we left the station at Worcester.'

'Perhaps there is snow on the line ahead of us,' suggested Crabb.

'Well, as soon as we arrive at Bromsgrove we will hire a cab to take us to the police station. I want to ask Bullman why his name is in Mr Stebbins's book. He must be able to tell us more about the old man's moneylending activities. After that I mean to go back to Bournheath. Perhaps Sir John may be more amenable to answering our questions today.'

'I hope so.'

There was a sudden shriek of brakes and both men were thrown forwards out of their seats.

'What the blazes!' exclaimed Ravenscroft as they picked themselves up. 'There must be something on the line.' He opening the window and strained to see up the side of the carriage. 'Strange. I would not have thought that the snow was deep enough to cause a problem.'

'Shall I go and have a look?' asked Crabb.

'Better not. It could be a false alarm, and we will move again soon. I believe I can see someone walking down the line towards us. I think it is the guard,' said Ravenscroft. 'Hello, my man! What is the trouble?'

'Body on the line, sir,' replied the guard.

'Good Lord! We are police officers.'

'Thank God, sir. We could do with your help.'

Ravenscroft quickly opened the carriage door and clambered out. The two detectives ran up to the front of the train, passing by a number of carriages where the passengers were looking out of their windows in an attempt to see what had caused the abrupt stop.

The engine driver, stoker and one or two of the other passengers were already gathered some twenty yards in front of the engine, looking down at the body on the tracks.

'It is alright, we are police officers,' shouted Ravenscroft as the driver turned to motion them not to come any nearer.

'I could see something on the line and pulled up sharp,' said the driver, visibly shaken.

'You did well. Let me see,' said Ravenscroft, kneeling down.

'Poor man!' muttered the guard.

'I think it would be better if you went back down the train to prevent anyone else from alighting,' instructed Ravenscroft addressing the guard.

'Yes, sir. Come away, now then, sir, madam,' replied the guard ushering the two onlookers away from the scene.

'Give me some assistance, Tom. I want to turn him over on his front,' said Ravenscroft. 'He seems to have sustained a nasty blow on the back of his head, and looks as though he has been dead for some hours. He must have lost a lot of blood. Driver, there must have been earlier trains than ours today?'

'No, sir. There were some services scheduled, but a signal failed just outside Worcester some hours ago. We are the first train through today,' replied the engine driver.

'But surely there would have been trains in the other direction?'

'They would have been told not to proceed beyond Bromsgrove because of the failure down our side of the line.'

'When was the last train yesterday evening?'

'Eleven thirty, sir,' replied the driver.

'He does not look as though he has been hit by a train. He must have been here all night. I noticed before we turned him over that his coat was partially covered in snow. How far are we from Bromsgrove Station?'

'About a quarter of a mile.'

'I would be obliged if you and Sergeant Crabb would assist me in moving the body to the side of the track. Then I suggest that you take the rest of the passengers on to Bromsgrove as soon as possible. Send someone to the police station in Bromsgrove, asking for Detective Inspector Bullman, and saying that we need urgent assistance. My sergeant and I will remain with the body until then.'

'Yes, sir.'

The three men lifted the body and moved it a small clearing at the side of the track.

'Thank you, Mr, er . . . ?'

'Perkins, sir.'

'Mr Perkins. As quick as you can, if you please.'

'Yes, sir,' replied the driver, running back towards the train.

'Take a quick look on the track, before he starts the engine, in case there is anything there that might have fallen out of the man's pockets,' instructed Ravenscroft.

'Nothing, sir,' said Crabb.

The two detectives watched as the train moved slowly along the track, many of its passengers looking out of the windows, and talking loudly, as they passed by.

'Now let us see who this poor unfortunate man is,' said Ravenscroft as the train disappeared from view round the next bend. 'I would say the deceased is about forty years of age, of average build, sporting a fine set of white side-whiskers, well dressed in suit and overcoat, wearing a red scarf around his neck. See what you can find in his pockets while I have a look at the sides of the track.'

'Nothing, sir,' said Crabb again, after Ravenscroft had returned from his examination of the surrounding locality. 'His pockets are completely empty, and there is also no name on the label at the back of the overcoat.'

'I think someone killed him. That is quite a blow at the back of his head, which would not have resulted from his merely falling over on to the track. Interestingly I found what looked like the signs of a horse-drawn conveyance of some sort still embedded in the snow. I think the dead man was brought here and left on the track sometime during the night, after the eleven thirty train had gone down.'

'But why would someone have gone to all that trouble? Why not just leave the body somewhere else?' asked Crabb.

'Because whoever killed him did not want to take the chance that the body would be found and a positive identification made. You noticed, did you not, that the deceased's head was positioned across the track? The killer left the body purposely on the track in the hope that the early train would run over it in the dark, so that the man would be disfigured beyond all recognition. I think our killer also wanted to make it look like this man had met with an accident, that he had fallen on the track and been rendered unconscious.'

'Horrible!' muttered Crabb.

'And the plan would have succeeded, had not that early-morning signal failure outside Worcester prevented trains from using the line. Ours was the first train to use the track today, and fortunately our driver could see clearly that there was something ahead of him, and managed to halt the train in time. I wonder who this poor fellow was, and why he was killed in such a cruel fashion.'

'What will we do now, sir?' saw Crabb, turning up his collar against the cold wind.

'There is nothing we can do, until Inspector Bullman arrives, which I hope will not be too long.'

* * *

'Inspector Bullman,' said Ravenscroft as the detective came striding up to the track, followed by two uniformed officers, and a number of railway workers pulling a large handcart.

'Inspector Ravenscroft,' acknowledged Bullman. 'Well, what have we got here?'

'Man found dead on the track,' replied Ravenscroft.

'Suicide, I'll be bound. There is usually one or two every few years. This one evidently could not face all the joys of the festive season.'

'He has been hit on the back of the head.'

'Could have been hit by a passing train,' suggested Bullman kneeling down to examine the body.

'The body was lying on the track itself, and has not been disfigured, which suggests it was placed here after the last train passed through at eleven thirty last night.'

'Oh? What about the morning trains?'

'We have established that our train was the first on the line this morning. A signal failure outside Worcester stopped them coming through till now.'

'It certainly looks nasty enough. We will see what the doctor has to say when they have taken a look at him at the mortuary. Right, you men, load him on to the cart. You know where to take him. Did he have any identification on him?'

'No, sir,' replied Crabb. 'Nor anything on the ground that I can find.'

'Not helpful. Not helpful at all, what with Christmas coming and all that. I guess we will have to leave this until after Christmas day. I've got too much on my hands at present. I have to appear in court at Worcester later this morning. Damned unhelpful coming at this time,' muttered Bullman.

'Crimes are never committed at times to suit our own personal convenience,' said Ravenscroft.

'Look here, Ravenscroft, what do you say if you take over this case, seeing as you found him and all that?' suggested Bullman.

'Well I don't know about that,' protested the detective.

'I would be mighty obliged.'

'It is not my jurisdiction.'

'Consider yourself authorised. You will be doing me a great favour. I'm terribly busy in Court, as I said, and you were first on the scene.'

'Well, I suppose we could make some enquiries.'

'Splendid. Good man. Keep me informed of developments.'

'Of course; that goes without saying.'

'What about this other business?'

'We are making good progress.'

'Good, but I tell you that lad is as guilty as a pickled onion about to be eaten.'

'I'm sure you are right,' replied Ravenscroft, forcing a brief smile.

'I will leave it to you. Good day to you, Ravenscroft. Come, men, back to the mortuary with him. Have a care there — we are not dealing with a sack of potatoes.'

Ravenscroft and Crabb watched as the policemen and railway men made their way down the track, pushing the handcart bearing the body in front of them.

'I cannot believe that I agreed to this investigation!' Ravenscroft sighed. 'Just when we are conducting enquiries into old Mr Stebbins's murder we are now faced with trying to find out who this dead man was, and who killed him. How can I have been so foolish to have agreed to Bullman's request?'

'There might be time to attend to both cases, sir,' said Crabb, trying to sound as hopeful as he could.

'We had better make a start. Those marks in the snow, by the side of the track — I am sure that they were made by some horse-drawn trap or similar means of transport.' Ravenscroft walked up the slope and on to the verge. 'If we follow these indentations in the snow, they may lead us somewhere.'

'It looks as though the vehicle turned here.' Crabb pointed to the ground.

'So the killer probably went back the same way as he came. It is fortunate for us that it stopped snowing shortly after the body had been left on the tracks. A further fall would have hidden all signs.'

Ravenscroft and Crabb followed the ruts in the snow for several minutes, until the track joined a wider road.

'We are out of luck. There is an indication that one or two other vehicles have also been this way this morning. It is impossible to say which one is our quarry. Damn!'

'What will we do now, sir?'

'I don't see that there is much more that we can do, other than issue a description of the dead man, and hope that someone will come forward to claim him. It might be worth our while making enquiries at the railway station, I suppose. It could be that the man was a stranger to the area, and that he might have arrived by train,' said a disappointed Ravenscroft.

The two men retraced their steps towards the train line, and followed the edge of the track towards the railway station.

Making their way directly on to the platform, Ravenscroft observed a tall, elderly stationmaster consulting a pocketbook.

'Good morning,' said Ravenscroft.

'Ah, you must be the policemen?' asked the stationmaster.

'We are.'

'This is a nasty business.'

'Indeed.'

'The policemen have taken the body away, and as you can see the train has continued on its way.'

'Good. I don't suppose you got a look at the dead man?'

'I did, sir, and it was not a pretty sight.'

'No. Do you think he was a local man?'

'He was not from around these parts.'

'Could he have been a passenger? I ask because he was on the railway track, and perhaps he had been visiting the area, and you might have seen him?' asked Ravenscroft, realising that he was clutching at straws.

'Why yes, sir.'

'You do remember him?'

'He arrived two days ago. I remember taking his ticket as he alighted from the train.'

'I don't suppose you recall where he came from?'

'Sorry, I just took his ticket. I do remember, though, that he asked where he could get a cab from.'

'And what did you say?' asked Ravenscroft, encouraged by the man's answers.

'I escorted him to the front of the station, and pointed him in the direction of old Judd, one of our cab drivers.'

'Excellent. Thank you, sir.'

'Glad to have been of help.'

Ravenscroft and Crabb made their way to the front of the building.

'There is a cab waiting over there,' said Crabb.

'Good day, would your name happen to be Judd?' asked Ravenscroft addressing a grizzled man, who was slumped in the seat of his cab.

'I might be; then again, I might not be. It all depends on who is asking, and whether you be a paying passenger or not,' muttered the cabman, scarcely looking up.

'I shall take that as a "yes." My name is Detective Inspector Ravenscroft. We may well require your services.'

'You something to do with that body on the line that left the station a while back?'

'We are investigating the death of the poor man. We understand from the stationmaster that he arrived in Bromsgrove two days ago, and that you may have taken him to his destination. He was a tall gentleman, white side-whiskers, wearing a long overcoat and a red scarf.'

'I remembers the scarf.'

'Can you recall where you took the gentleman?'

'I took him to the Black Cross in Bromsgrove.'

'Excellent. We would be obliged if you could take us there now.'

'Climb inside.' Judd suddenly roused himself and took hold of his whip in one hand.

The two detectives entered the cab, which set off at a brisk pace, travelling along a number of roads and then down a hill, towards the centre of the town, before turning left and eventually pulling up outside an old coaching inn.

'Thank you, Judd.' Ravenscroft handed the cabman a coin.

'Hope you enjoys your stay there. Mind how you go. Look out for that old cavalier.' Judd bit on the coin.

'What old cavalier?' asked Ravenscroft, puzzled.

'You'll see!' laughed the cabman, cracking his whip again. The cab lurched forwards and set off down the road.

'I don't know what the old man was talking about.' Ravenscroft pushed open the door of the inn.

'He's been out too long in the cold,' agreed Crabb.

The two detectives found themselves in a dimly lit room, with oak panelling and a plastered ceiling, with an old view of the town on one of the walls and a reception desk at the far end.

'There seems to be no one here.'

'Good morning,' said a stocky middle-aged Irishman, with untidy hair and a broad grin, suddenly rising from behind the desk. 'Now I can see that you two gentlemen are in need of rooms for the night, and a glass of our best ale, if I am not mistaken.'

'Alas, no, but I thank you for your offer.'

'Well that would be a pity, would it not? I can assure you that you will not find more comfortable beds in the whole of Bromsgrove, nor will you be any more successful in obtaining a better glass of ale in the town than at the Black Cross.'

'I understand that a gentleman arrived here two days ago — a tall gentleman with white side-whiskers, wearing a long overcoat and a red scarf?' asked Ravenscroft.

'Ah well now, I wonder why you would be asking about him?' replied the innkeeper, giving the policemen a cautious look.

'My name is Detective Inspector Ravenscroft. This is my colleague, Detective Sergeant Crabb. We are making enquiries about this gentleman, and our cabman has informed us that he dropped off his fare here two days ago.'

'Ah well now, that is an interesting thing. I thought to myself when I saw you entering the Black Cross, sure as twelve pennies make a shilling, that you were men of law and order, and that, as Detective Inspector Bullman and some of his associates are already good customers here, you could not be from this part of the county.'

'We are based at Ledbury,' offered Crabb.

'Ledbury, you say. Well that is a fine thing — it was only last year that my wife and I took the train to Ledbury, and I remember saying to Mrs Symonds what a remarkable town it was, with all those fine buildings, and that castle on the top of the hill. To be sure, it was a fine town, indeed.'

'I think you must be mistaken; Ledbury does not have a castle, although it does have many fine buildings,' corrected Ravenscroft.

'Is that so? Well it must have been somewhere else that we went to. Would you believe it? The memory plays fine tricks, does it not? I wonder where we might have visited that day.'

'I would be grateful if we could return to the matter in hand,' said Ravenscroft. 'The gentleman in the long overcoat and red scarf — did he arrive here two days ago?'

'Ah, to be sure he did. He took one of our finest rooms he did, although the gentleman did not know how long he would be staying with us.'

'That is interesting. Did he sign your register?' asked Ravenscroft.

'Ah, to be sure, he did.'

'Then I would be obliged if we could see the entry.'

'Well now, I wonder why you might be a-wanting to do that for. Surely if this man is known to your good selves, then you must also be familiar with the said gentleman's name.'

'Mr Symonds, may I remind you that we are police officers.' Ravenscroft was beginning to tire of the landlord's roundabout way of talking. 'We do not have time for all of this. We are investigating the death of this man, whose body was found on the railway line near Bromsgrove Station. He had no identification on his person. That is why we need to see your register, if you please.'

'Well now, is that not a terrible thing to have happened? Mrs Symonds and I were just wondering why the gentleman had not come down for his breakfast this morning, and I said to Mrs Symonds—'

'Yes, thank you. The register, if you please,' interrupted Ravenscroft, raising his voice and drumming his fingers on the counter in annoyance.

Symonds said nothing as he dropped down from view, reappearing a few seconds later brandishing a large leather-bound volume.

'Thank you.' Ravenscroft turned over the pages until he arrived at the last few entries. 'Which would be the correct name?'

'Well, that would be the last but one.'

'Mr Eustace Conningsby.'

'That will be the one, to be sure.'

'Did this Mr Conningsby give any indication where he had come from?'

'Well now, he might have done, and there again he might not.'

'Mr Symonds, did he, or did he not, say where he came from?' asked Ravenscroft, feeling himself becoming more and more annoyed by the man's ambivalence.

'Let me see. Yes. London. I do believe he said he came from London.'

'This is not very helpful,' said a dispirited Crabb.

'While Mr Conningsby was staying with you did he happen to mention the reason for his visit?'

'I do not believe that he did.'

'Did he meet anyone while he was here?'

'Well now, let me see, there was no one that I recall. He dined alone.'

'When was the last time you saw him?'

'Yesterday evening. He dined about eight, sat in the snug until eleven, then he went out.'

'Did he say where he was going?'

'No, I do not believe that he did.'

'And you did not see him return?'

'No, that is correct; I did not see him return.'

'Was it snowing heavily last night?'

'Now, then, I can see that you have a keen brain to be asking the right questions. I think you might be right on that score.'

'Did you not think it strange that a man should be going outside in such inclement weather, and at such a late hour?'

'Well now that you come to think of it, I did consider it rather odd at the time.'

'And you did not think it strange when he did not appear for breakfast this morning?'

'To be sure I did, but then I thought he must have come back in the middle of the night, and that he was still sleeping.'

'Would not the inn door have been locked?'

'Ah, to be sure it was.'

'Then how could he have got in?'

'That is a good question, but to answer you — he had a key. All our guests have keys.'

'Well quite clearly he did not come back here in the middle of the night, or earlier this morning, as by then he was already dead and lying on the railway line. Mr Symonds, I would like to see Mr Conningsby's room, if you please.'

'Well now, I am not sure if that would be possible.'

'Oh, and why is that?'

'If the said gentleman is no longer with us, then he will not be requiring his room.'

'That is correct.'

'And if he no longer requires the room, then Mrs Symonds will be a-wanting to make it ready for the next guest.'

'Mr Symonds, may I remind you that one of your guests has been killed in a most cruel way, and that we are police officers making urgent enquiries into this case. It is therefore imperative that we examine the room,' said Ravenscroft, aware that he was raising his voice once again.

'Ah well, you should have said that in the first place,' replied Symonds, removing a key from a board behind him.

Ravenscroft and Crabb followed the innkeeper up a flight of stairs and along a narrow passageway.

'The gentleman was staying here in Room 2. To be sure, it is just as the man left it.' Symonds opened the door and cast a brief glance round the room.

'I would be obliged if you would leave us now. My colleague and I wish to make a thorough search of Mr Conningsby's effects.'

Symonds said nothing as he stood by the door, seeming reluctant to comply with Ravenscroft's request.

'Thank you, Mr Symonds. We will let you know when we are done,' said the detective in a firm voice.

'Well then, I'll be leaving you two good souls to it, then,' the innkeeper replied before finally leaving the room and closing the door behind him.

'What an insufferable man,' whispered Ravenscroft.

'He seemed very reluctant to give a straight answer to a straight question,' agreed Crabb.

'Now then, Tom, let us see what we can find out about our mysterious Eustace Conningsby. There is a holdall at the foot of the bed,' said Ravenscroft. 'See if any of his clothes are in the wardrobe, and if so check all the pockets.'

'Yes, sir.'

'The holdall is empty; now for the chest of drawers. It looks as though our Mr Conningsby travelled lightly. It contains only two pairs of socks.'

'Only a spare jacket in here, pockets empty, and two shirts,' added Crabb.

'He certainly liked to travel unencumbered. His wardrobe suggests that he did not intend to stay for long. It looks as though we are not going to find out anything about this man from his wardrobe,' remarked Ravenscroft, finding it difficult to hide his disappointment. 'What the devil brought him to Bromsgrove, I wonder? Why did he go out at such a late hour? And why was he killed?'

'There is a Bible on the table by the side of the bed,' Crabb pointed out.

'Probably belongs to the management.' Ravenscroft picked up the book. 'Ah no, here is the man's name, Eustace Conningsby, written on the inside flyleaf.'

'At least we now know that was his real name.'

'We do indeed.' Ravenscroft held the book by its spine and shook it to see if there was anything loose within its pages. 'What is this? It looks like a letter. Let us see what it says.

'Bromsgrove. 15 December.

'My dear sir,

'I thank you for your letter of the tenth.

'If you would care to visit me here in Bromsgrove on the twenty-first, we may then be able to proceed further with this matter. I have the required document in my possession.

'Your obedient servant.'

'How interesting,' said Crabb, when Ravenscroft had finished reading the letter.

'Yes. What a pity the letter is unsigned; it would have been useful if we knew who sent it to Conningsby. It is very formal in tone. The paper is plain, of a cheap variety.'

'So that was what brought him to Bromsgrove.'

'It would appear so. Let us go through what we know. Conningsby arrived here two days ago, when I presume that he met the writer of the letter, but having done so he remained in the town instead of returning to London, went out in the snow late yesterday evening, probably to meet someone, and was then killed, his corpse being placed on the railway line, in the hope that no identification would be possible,' said Ravenscroft, thinking out loud.

'Poor man,' remarked Crabb.

'The letter says, "We may be able to proceed further with this matter. I have the required document in my possession." What document? And how would it have helped them to proceed further? Further with what? It is a great shame that the letter is not more comprehensive. Nor is there an envelope with it, which would have helped us with Conningsby's address. I wonder who he went out to meet yesterday evening. This case certainly grows more intriguing by the minute, but I fear I cannot see how we can proceed further at this present time. We don't know the dead man's address, or who wrote him the letter, or what this great matter was that encouraged him to come here. We will just have to put all this on one side for now. I think we should return to our original investigation into who killed old Mr Stebbins.'

'What will we do next then, sir?'

'I think the answer to this crime lies with the old man's moneylending activities. We know that he lent money to both Sir John Critchwood and Peter Nightingale. I would like to know more about their activities. Nightingale first.'

* * *

As the two detectives made their way up New Road, they turned their collars up against the falling snow, which was now slowly beginning to cover the streets and pavements of the town.

Ravenscroft rang the bell, and was surprised by how quickly the door opened.

'Christopher — oh, I'm sorry,' said Mary Nightingale.

'Good day to you, Miss Nightingale. I am sorry if you were expecting someone else,' smiled Ravenscroft. 'I wonder whether we might have a few more words with your brother.'

'I am afraid my brother is presently not at home,' remarked Mary Nightingale.

'Can you tell us when you might expect his return?'

'I believe he will be away for some hours. He has business to attend to before Christmas.'

'Then perhaps you might be willing to assist us with our enquiries.'

'I do not think so. I am sure that my brother has told you everything already regarding his association with Mr Stebbins.'

'Our investigation into the poor unfortunate man's death has brought to light further lines of enquiry, which we are forced to pursue with the utmost urgency. Another man's life may well depend on it,' said Ravenscroft, seeking to break through the woman's icy exterior. 'I can assure you that we will not take up more of your time than is absolutely necessary.'

Mary Nightingale said nothing, as she stared into the distance with a worn, expressionless look on her face.

'Miss Nightingale,' repeated Ravenscroft, uncomfortable at the other's apparent indifference.

'Yes, I am sorry, you had better come in. This way.' She led them to the same room they had been received in upon their previous visit. 'Please be seated.'

'Thank you, Miss Nightingale. When we interviewed your brother yesterday, he informed us that he was in the habit of purchasing books from Mr Stebbins.'

'That is correct.' Mary clasped her hands tightly together in her lap.

'Did your brother ever borrow money from Mr Stebbins?'

'No. Why would he need to borrow money from such a man?'

'We found this notebook amongst Mr Stebbins's possessions. It contains a list of names, each of whom borrowed money from him. It transpires that Mr Stebbins was also a moneylender in addition to his role as a bookseller. Your brother's name occurs more than once in the book.'

'This is quite absurd. My brother has no need to borrow money from anyone. We live a frugal existence and Peter's work as an insurance agent provides us with an additional income to the existing annuity which our late father left us.'

'So you have no knowledge of these loans?'

'I have just said that my brother has no need for such recourse.'

'Forgive me, Miss Nightingale, if I bring up a rather delicate matter,' said Ravenscroft hesitantly. 'Your brother mentioned that your illness required the payment of medical bills. Might not your brother have needed such sums of money for those payments?'

'I am sure not. It is true that I have not been well of late, and at present I am undertaking a course of medication, but I can assure you that we have more than enough funds for that.'

Ravenscroft observed that his last question had caused a degree of unease, as Mary Nightingale gripped her fingers tightly in her lap, and her complexion assumed an even greyer hue.

'Thank you, Miss Nightingale.'

'I cannot understand what all this has to do with Peter. He only ever purchased books from Mr Stebbins. I am sure of that. We had no social contact with the man.'

'Does your brother know Sir John Critchwood?' asked Ravenscroft, deciding to change his line of questioning.

'Everyone in Bromsgrove knows of the Critchwood family. They are, I believe, wealthy landowners. I think they live somewhere near Finstall.'

'Bournheath,' corrected Ravenscroft.

'Bournheath. Yes, of course.'

'Old Dodford Manor. My colleague and I visited there yesterday. Sir John was conducting a meeting. I noticed that one of the men, seated around the table at that meeting was your brother.' Ravenscroft observed her closely for any reaction that his words might create. 'Could you possibly tell me what the meeting was about?'

'I know nothing of such a meeting. I was not aware that my brother even knew Sir John Critchwood.' Mary Nightingale sounded defensive.

'Did your brother ever talk to you about the Critchwood family?'

'No, never. As I have previously stated, we have no special social contact with the Critchwood family.'

'Does the name Eustace Conningsby mean anything to you?'

'No,' replied Mary Nightingale, but there was a catch in her voice. 'Why do you ask?'

'Mr Conningsby's body was found this morning, on the railway track just outside Bromsgrove.'

'Oh!' exclaimed Mary Nightingale.

'Miss Nightingale, are you unwell?' asked Ravenscroft.

'I'm sorry, you must forgive me. Your words bought back painful memories. Many years ago, a dear friend of mine fell on to the railway line and was killed,' said Mary, struggling to regain her composure.

'Can I get you a glass of water?'

'No, I am well now.'

'I am sorry. I did not wish to cause you any distress. Sergeant Crabb and I will take our leave. Thank you for your assistance.'

The two detectives followed the lady of the house into the hall.

Mary Nightingale opened the front door and Ravenscroft and Crabb stepped out on to the pavement.

'She is lying, of course,' said Ravenscroft, as they walked away from the house. 'She knows Eustace Conningsby. Did you see how upset she became when I informed her of Conningsby's death? I thought for a moment that she was going to faint, but then she quickly recovered, and gave us all that nonsense about a friend of hers who died on the railway tracks.'

'That wasn't the only thing she was lying about. She pretended that she did not know anything about the Critchwood family, even saying she thought they came from Finstall.'

'So you noticed that as well, Tom. She was trying to stop us gaining the truth. And when we arrived did you see how quickly she opened the door. She was clearly expecting someone else. Quickly, Tom, into this doorway!' instructed Ravenscroft, moving swiftly to the side of the street. 'Look. If I am not mistaken that is Christopher Critchwood knocking on the Nightingales' door.'

'She called out the name "Christopher" when we arrived,' added Crabb.

As the two detectives watched, the door of the house was quickly opened by Mary Nightingale. She reached out and clasped the shoulder of the new arrival, before he quickly stepped inside.

'So it was Mr Critchwood that Mary Nightingale was expecting. How old would you say that Miss Nightingale was?'

'About thirty-five,' answered Crabb.

'I am inclined to agree, although a prolonged illness can age one by some years. And what would you say was the age of Mr Critchwood?'

'I would think that he is between twenty and twenty-five years of age.'

'Yes. They seem an unlikely match, both in years and temperament. I wonder what ails Mary Nightingale? There was no coughing, or difficulty in breathing, but quite clearly the woman is suffering from some long-term illness. Her movements are slow, her face lined, complexion pale, and beneath that distant and worn exterior I see anxiety and a quiet pain.'

'I wonder if Mr Nightingale knows of his sister's association with young Mr Critchwood?'

'Perhaps not. That may be why he called on the lady during her brother's absence.'

'Shall I call a cab, sir?'

'Yes, indeed. It is time that we paid Sir John Critchwood another visit.'

CHAPTER FOUR

BOURNHEATH

'It will be interesting to see what Sir John has to tell us about the money he borrowed from old Mr Stebbins,' said Ravenscroft as he and Crabb sat in the back of old Judd's cab. 'I hope he is more open to questions now that his "important meeting" is over.'

Suddenly the cab came to a violent halt, flinging Ravenscroft and Crabb abruptly to one side.

'What the devil!' exclaimed Ravenscroft throwing open the cab door and looking anxiously all around him.

'Sorry, sir. I had to swerve to avoid the post boy,' said Judd, steadying the horse.

Ravenscroft and Crabb jumped out and ran back down the road to where a young man dressed in a postman's uniform was engaged in clambering out of a ditch.

'Are you alright?'

'Yes, thank you. I didn't see the horse coming round the corner.' The post boy had regained his footing and was brushing the snow off his uniform.

'Are you injured in any way?' asked Crabb.

'No, sir. I am sorry to have caused such trouble. I hope no one is hurt.'

'No, don't worry yourself on that count. Just one alarmed horse, thank you Mr—'

'Jelps, sir. I am employed at the Bromsgrove Post Office. I had just been delivering the post to Old Dodford Manor.'

'Well, Mr Jelps it is good to see that no harm has been done to either party. It is a terrible day to be out in all this snow,' said Ravenscroft.

'It is indeed, sir. I shall be glad when I have returned to Bromsgrove, but I have letters to deliver first in the village,' replied the boy, giving a large grin.

'I wish you well, Jelps. Take care,' said Ravenscroft as he and Crabb made their way back towards the cab.

'A happy Christmas to you, sir,' shouted the post boy as he picked up his sack of mail.

'And to you,' called out Crabb as he and Ravenscroft climbed into the cab.

'Onward!' instructed Ravenscroft tapping his fist on the side of the vehicle. 'Well, Tom,' he said, rubbing his elbow, 'that is the second time today we've been thrown out of our seats. Bromsgrove at Christmastime is a hazardous place for both of us.'

'More hazardous for Mr Conningsby than for us,' remarked Crabb.

A minute or two later they alighted from the cab outside the main door of Old Dodford Manor.

'I would be obliged if you would remain here during our visit. I have no doubt that we will have need of your services again.' Ravenscroft handed a silver coin to the cabman.

'You best be quick then,' mumbled old Judd, giving the detective a look of indifference. 'At the rate this snow is falling you won't be travelling very much further today.'

'I am sure that the horse can manage quite well.'

'He might, but I could find it difficult.'

'Then here is another coin for your troubles,' said Ravenscroft.

'I knew you were a gentleman when I first saw you, sir,' grinned Judd, eagerly accepting the coin.

'It looks as though someone has noticed our arrival,' said Crabb.

'Ah, good morning to you, Mr March,' said Ravenscroft as the agent came down the front steps.

'What do you want here?' demanded March in a none too civil manner.

'I was hoping to have another word with Sir John.'

'Sir John answered all your questions yesterday. There is nothing else he can add.'

'With all due respect, that is for Sir John to tell us.'

'And I am telling you, with all due respect, that you are not wanted here,' growled March.

'May I remind you, Mr March, that we are police officers, and that it is an offence to obstruct a policeman in the carrying out of his lawful duty. If you persist in blocking our attempt to interview Sir John, then I will have little recourse but to arrest you and take you to Bromsgrove Police Station for further questioning. I am sure that Sir John would be far from happy to learn of that situation.'

The two men eyed one another in complete silence.

'Sir John, or the handcuffs — which is it? Crabb, the handcuffs, if you please,' instructed Ravenscroft.

'Alright, wait here.' March sighed reluctantly before striding back up the steps.

'If you asks me, them Critchwoods has got above themselves,' laughed Judd.

'No one asked you,' retorted Ravenscroft, walking away from the cab.

'Sir John still may refuse to see us,' said Crabb.

'Oh, I don't think he will. One thing the gentry dislike is any hint of scandal,' remarked Ravenscroft, pacing up and down the path.

Presently the front door of the house opened again, and March curtly beckoned the two men forwards. 'Sir John can spare you five minutes of his time, in his study, but that is all.'

Ravenscroft and Crabb followed the agent and soon found themselves entering a book-lined room. Sir John Critchwood was seated behind a desk at the far end reading some papers.

'Sit down,' he said, without looking up.

'It is good of you to see us again, Sir John. I realise your time is important—'

'I doubt if you have any notion of how valuable my time may or may not be,' interrupted Sir John.

'It is about the entry in Mr Stebbins's notebook.'

'I told you yesterday that I know nothing about such an entry.'

'Two hundred and fifty pounds; that is a large sum of money,' continued Ravenscroft, determined that now he had come this far he would not be intimidated by the landowner.

'If I wanted that sort of money I would have borrowed it from the bank, not from some backstreet moneylender,' snapped Sir John. He leaned back in his chair and glared at Ravenscroft.

'That is what I would have thought, but why would old Stebbins have included your name in his account book?'

'Fantasy. Some men are dreamers and will make up all kinds of nonsense in their spare time. Now if that is all . . .'

'Do you know Peter Nightingale, Sir John?' asked Ravenscroft quickly changing the subject matter of his questioning.

'I may have had one or two minor dealings with the gentleman in question over the years. Why do you ask?'

'It is only that when I visited you yesterday, I thought I observed that Mr Nightingale was one of the gentlemen seated at your table.'

'You must have been mistaken. I have only met Mr Nightingale once or twice before. He was not at our meeting yesterday. Now if you will excuse me.'

'May I ask the nature of your meeting?' continued Ravenscroft tentatively, telling himself that he would be surprised if he received a satisfactory reply to his question.

'It was a board meeting of the Bromsgrove Gas Light and Coke Company. I am its chairman. The directors meet twice a year to authorise accounts and plan future investment.'

'I see. Does the name Eustace Conningsby mean anything to you?'

'No. I cannot say that I have ever heard of the man. Why do you ask?'

'Mr Conningsby's body was found on the railway line, just outside Bromsgrove Station, earlier this morning. He had been murdered. We found a letter amongst his possessions, asking him to come to the town,' said Ravenscroft with emphasis, watching closely for any change in Sir John's manner.

'As I said, I do not know the man. I don't know what all of this has to do with me. I believe our business is now completed, Inspector. I am a busy man. March, show them out,' ordered Sir John, before looking down at his papers again and taking up his pen.

* * *

'Do you believe him, sir?' asked Crabb, as the two men walked down the steps.

'No. When I mentioned Conningsby's name I detected just a slight hint of recognition, before he quickly corrected himself, and denied all knowledge of the poor man.'

'Perhaps it was Sir John who wrote that letter to Conningsby,' suggested Crabb.

'And I am sure he did borrow that money from Mr Stebbins, despite his denial. The house looks well enough, but you never know how much in debt these landowners actually are. Everything might look very fine on the outside, but a man's wealth can have easily been funded by debts and loans that can never be repaid. And I know that it was Peter Nightingale I saw yesterday at that board meeting. Why lie about that? It is arrogance itself to suggest a detective inspector should not believe the evidence of his own eyes.'

'You think that Nightingale and Sir John are working together, and that they could both be involved in the deaths of old Mr Stebbins and Eustace Conningsby?'

'I don't know at this stage. It may be that we are dealing with two different crimes. We only happen to be asking these people about Conningsby because we are interviewing them anyway and have no other leads. I don't want to force any connections between the two, when in all probability there aren't any. I must say, though, that this Bromsgrove Gas Light and Coke Company interests me. As does Sir John Critchwood's involvement.'

Judd was shivering when they finally turned to him. 'Where do you want to go to now, Inspector?' He brushed the snow from his large overcoat.

'Which is the main bank in town?'

'Oh, that will be the old Worcester City and County Bank. The others aren't up to much.'

'Then I would like you to take us there,' instructed Ravenscroft, climbing into the cab.

'Right you are.'

* * *

The bank occupied a large half-timbered property at the bottom of New Road. It was warm inside and quiet as a library; a solitary clerk scratched numbers into a ledger behind the desk.

'Good afternoon, my man,' Ravenscroft said to the bank clerk. 'I would be obliged if we could have a few words with the manager, if you please.'

'Do you have an account with us, sir?'

'No.'

'Thinking of opening an account?'

'No.'

'Then I do not think it will be possible for you to see Mr Fitzwilliam today,' replied the clerk, peering down at the two detectives through his thick-lensed spectacles with a look of disdain.

'We are police officers. Perhaps you would be kind enough to give Mr Fitzwilliam my card, and say to him that it is imperative that we speak to him on a matter of urgency.'

The clerk hesitated for a moment, and then accepting Ravenscroft's card loudly closed his partition, and walked off into the back room.

'My dear Inspector Ravenscroft, a matter of the gravest urgency?' said an elderly, cheery-faced man emerging forth shortly from the inner room.

'It is indeed, Mr Fitzwilliam,' said Ravenscroft in the most serious voice he could muster.

'Then you had better follow me, yes you better had.'

Ravenscroft and Crabb followed the manager into the inner office.

'Please do take a seat. Now how can I be of assistance to you both? The whole of the expertise of the Worcester City and County Bank is at your service, indeed it is,' said Fitzwilliam, busily tidying the contents of his desk.

'We are at present investigating the death of Mr Stebbins, the bookseller. Do you know of the gentleman?' asked Ravenscroft.

'I do indeed. Mr Stebbins is, or rather was, one of our customers.'

'I wonder if you could enlighten us as to the gentleman's financial position.'

'I am afraid that would be totally unethical of the bank to disclose the financial affairs of one of its clients, yes it is.'

'But Mr Stebbins is dead, so surely there is no confidentially involved,' suggested Ravenscroft.

'Well.'

'And we are police officers, and an innocent man's life lies in the balance.'

'Yes, well, yes — an innocent man, you say? I see. I suppose in this case it will do no harm. Mr Stebbins is dead, as you say, dead, indeed.' As he spoke, Fitzwilliam continued fussily rearranging his papers on his desk. 'Mr Stebbins currently has approaching nearly two thousand pounds in his account.'

'Good heavens!' exclaimed Crabb.

'That is rather a lot of money, if I may say so, and I don't think it could have all come from the sale of second-hand books,' remarked Ravenscroft.

'Indeed not.'

'Was the bank aware that Mr Stebbins was also a moneylender?'

'He never intimated as such, but I believe that we had our suspicions, yes I believe we did.' Fitzwilliam removed his spectacles and began to clean them vigorously on a large yellow cloth.

'We found this book in his premises; it contains details of all of his financial transactions.'

'My word, what a state of affairs!'

'One of the names included in the book is that of Sir John Critchwood. Can you tell me whether this gentleman is one of your clients?'

'He is, indeed.'

'Sir John appears to have borrowed the sum of two hundred and fifty pounds from Mr Stebbins. Did he approach the bank first with such a request?' asked Ravenscroft.

'I am afraid that I cannot disclose the financial affairs of one of our current clients,' answered Fitzwilliam, shuffling uncomfortably in his chair, and looking down at his papers in a nervous manner.

'Of course, I appreciate your discretion, but I have to ask these questions, Mr Fitzwilliam, because if we are to bring the perpetrator of this crime to justice, we must learn the truth. Now, I would not expect you to disclose the full details of Sir John's account, but I would be obliged if you could answer my original question — did Sir John request such a loan from the bank?'

'Yes,' said Fitzwilliam reluctantly.

'And what was the outcome of that request?'

'The bank unfortunately had to decline such a loan at this time, yes, decline it we did.'

'Why was that?'

'It was not thought appropriate in this case. Sir John already owes the bank a considerable sum of money, and the directors of the bank considered that in this case it was not expedient to extend his overdraft facilities.'

'How much is Sir John in debt to the bank?'

'That I am not at liberty to say, but I can tell you that it is not an insubstantial sum, no indeed it is not.'

'If Sir John does not repay the bank, what could be the outcome?'

'The bank would insist on calling in the debt. That would mean that Old Dodford Manor and its contents would have to be sold to reimburse the bank — but I should add that there is no recourse to do that at present. Sir John is currently repaying his debts, on a monthly basis, and I have no doubt that in the fullness of time the balance will be repaid.'

'So that was why Sir John went to Mr Stebbins,' remarked Crabb.

'So it would appear, yes, indeed.'

'I appreciate your candour in this delicate matter. We understand that Sir John is the chairman of the Bromsgrove Gas Light and Coke Company.'

'That is indeed so.'

'Can you enlighten us further as to the activities of this company?'

'Well, yes, I suppose I might be able to throw a little light on its affairs, if you will excuse the jest. The company was formed in 1882. It supplies most of the gas and coal to the citizens of Bromsgrove and the surrounding areas.'

'Does the company have an account with your bank?'

'It does.'

'And is the company in credit?'

'Marginally so, as the company is always extending its reach to the outlying parts of the town, so its initial income from customers at this present time meets any debts it may have.'

'So Sir John would not have been able to draw on the company for his new loan?'

'I do not think so. The company's financial standing would be compromised, and it would be unethical for its chairman to raise a personal loan by such means, indeed it would.'

'Thank you, Mr Fitzwilliam, you have been extremely helpful to us,' said Ravenscroft.

'I am glad that I have been of assistance,' smiled the bank manager.

'Oh, just one more question. Does the name Eustace Conningsby mean anything to you?'

'Conningsby? Conningsby? The name does perhaps sound familiar, but . . . no, I cannot quite place it,' replied Fitzwilliam scratching his head. 'No, I do not recall the name.'

'So he could not have been one of your clients?'

'No, I would have recognised the name had Mr Conningsby had an account with us. No, I'm afraid the name means nothing to me.'

'May I ask that if you do remember the name, we would be obliged if you would leave a message for us at Bromsgrove Police Station,' said Ravenscroft.

'I don't suppose Sir John happened to mention what he wanted that loan for — the two hundred and fifty pounds?'

'Why, yes. It was for the purchase of land in the Charford area of Bromsgrove.'

'Why was Sir John desirous of undertaking this purchase?' asked Ravenscroft.

'I believe that Sir John had formed a new company with the express purpose of purchasing land in Charford for the building of a great many houses. Sir John showed me the plans, and very fine they were as well. There must have been well over a hundred houses. It seemed a very ambitious project. There is quite a demand for new homes in the town and its surrounding areas, indeed there is.'

'That is most interesting, Mr Fitzwilliam. I imagine that such a scheme would meet with universal approval in the town.'

'You would have thought so, but Mr Troth was violently opposed to the scheme.'

'Why was that?'

'Mr David Troth owns a large pig farm, which is situated in the middle of the proposed development. He is naturally opposed to any building in the area. Sir John assured me, however, that such opposition could be overcome.'

'And I presume that if the development went ahead, then Sir John stood to make a great deal of money,' suggested Ravenscroft.

'Indeed. But his arguments did not persuade our directors upon this occasion, owing to his already mounting debts.'

'That is all most interesting. I wish you good day, Mr Fitzwilliam,' said Ravenscroft.

'May I be so bold as to wish you both the compliments of the season?' smiled Fitzwilliam.

'And a happy Christmas to you, too.'

'Well that was all very informative,' said Crabb, as he and Ravenscroft made their way out of the bank.

'Yes. Sir John, unable to acquire two hundred and fifty pounds from the bank for his building project, went to Mr Stebbins to raise the money,' replied Ravenscroft.

'Do you think he could have killed the old man so that he would not have to repay the debt?'

'That could have been a possibility. In the meantime I think we should investigate this building scheme in more detail.'

'I suppose you'll be a-wanting to go somewhere else now?' muttered a bleary-eyed Judd as they approached the cab.

'Yes, please. You know of a Mr David Troth?' asked Ravenscroft.

'Which one do you want? Half the town is called Troth,' replied the cabman.

'I believe he owns a pig farm out at Charford.'

'Oh, that miserable old devil. What do you want with him?'

'That is our business. Will you take us there or not?' said Ravenscroft, anxious not to be thwarted in this new enterprise.

'It's still snowing; road will be difficult.'

'Will this help?' Ravenscroft handed the old cabman another shilling. 'And another one to bring us back.'

'Get in, governor.'

* * *

Charford was beyond the southern end of the town, the horse making heavy work of its journey through the ever-deepening snow, and the old cabman straining to see his way between the falling flakes.

Presently as the road gave way to a rutted track across a large field, they arrived outside an old decaying half-timbered house, which was surrounded on three sides by a number of barns in varying stages of disrepair, and a number of animal enclosures.

'You can smell the stench of the pigs from here!' exclaimed Crabb, wrinkling his nose up as the two detectives alighted from the cab.

'Surely you cannot object to such a noble animal, Tom,' joked Ravenscroft. 'You always told me that you have been born and raised on a farm.'

'Not one that had those revolting creatures. We only grew crops and had a few hens.'

'What the blazes are you doing out here on my land!' shouted a figure, waving a shotgun, suddenly emerging from one of the outbuildings.

'We are looking for Mr David Troth,' said Ravenscroft.

'Well you've found him.' As the stocky farmer came closer they saw he had a large red weal down the side of his face, and that his clothes were torn and dirty in appearance. 'Get off my land before I have the law on you. I suppose that Critchwood blackguard sent you. Well, you can tell him I am not moving and that's that!' growled Troth levelling the gun at Ravenscroft.

'We *are* the law,' declared Ravenscroft. 'And Sir John did not send us.'

'No matter, you get off my land.'

'I suggest you put down that shotgun before someone gets hurt. We only want to ask you a few questions,' Ravenscroft persisted, wondering whether the farmer would respond favourably to his demand, or decide to fire and ask questions afterwards. 'Not something worth hanging for, surely.'

'Sorry, I thought you were from that damned Critchwood.' Troth lowered his gun. 'Damn silly day to be out here.'

'We are investigating the death of Mr Stebbins, the old bookseller in Bromsgrove.' Ravenscroft was relieved that the danger was over, and anxious to proceed with his questions as quickly as he could.

'Never heard of him, but then I never goes into Bromsgrove,' muttered Troth, wiping a stained hand across his mouth.

'What can you tell us about Sir John?'

'Why, what's that blackguard been up to now?'

'I understand that Sir John wants to build a hundred houses on these fields,' continued Ravenscroft, looking casually around him.

'Over my dead body.' Troth spat on to the snow. 'We Troths have been farming here for the past three hundred years, or more, and we are not going to leave now! Critchwood may have bought up all the land around us, but he is not having my farm, and that's that.'

'I believe Sir John has offered you a great deal of money?' asked Crabb.

'He has. Two hundred pounds!'

'That must be very tempting. It is surely considerably more than the land is worth,' suggested Ravenscroft.

'Tempting or not, no Critchwood is going to build his houses on my land. All the others around here have taken their thirty pieces of silver, but we Troths are made of sterner stuff and are not for sale.'

'I don't suppose Sir John has taken too kindly to your refusal to sell?'

'He offered me fifty pounds at first, thought he would get it on the cheap. Then he increased his offer to a hundred, then a hundred and twenty. When I still said no, he said he would make me a final offer of two hundred pounds, but I told him I wasn't interested.'

'When was that?' asked Ravenscroft.

'That were about a month ago. Then last week he sent March and his men around to try and persuade me, but I gave them as much as they did,' laughed Troth, tapping the weal on his face with a grubby finger.

'So you would not go, even if Sir John offered you more money?'

'Never. What would I do anyway with two hundred pound? What would I do all day without my farm to look after? Now, is that all? I has to feed these pigs before nightfall, and if you want to get back to the town before you gets snowed in, then you best make tracks.'

'Indeed, thank you, Mr Troth. I don't suppose the name Conningsby, Mr Eustace Conningsby, means anything to you?' said Ravenscroft.

'I've never heard of him.'

'Thank you again.'

'And if you sees that Critchwood, you tell him from me that if any of his men sets foot on my land, I will blow their brains out!' growled Troth, brandishing his shotgun again.

'As a police officer I have to warn you against such drastic measures,' shouted Ravenscroft, as he and Crabb began to climb back inside the cab.

'Why? Are you going to protect me from that rogue Critchwood?' laughed Troth, banging the gate of one of the enclosures.

'To the railway station, if you please,' instructed Ravenscroft.

'You'll be lucky,' muttered Judd.

CHAPTER FIVE

BROMSGROVE

'What do you mean the train isn't running? My colleague and I must return to Ledbury immediately,' said Ravenscroft.

'I am sorry, but the line is completely blocked with snow further down the track, and is likely to get worse. I doubt that any train will get either in, or out of, Worcester today,' replied the stationmaster shaking his head.

'What are we going to do now?' Crabb didn't hide his disappointment.

'Damned infernal weather!' grumbled Ravenscroft walking away in annoyance. 'Well, there is nothing else for it, we will have to spend the night in Bromsgrove, and hope that the roads and railway lines are clearer tomorrow.'

They made for Judd's cab.

'Reckons you will be wanting rooms for the night at the Black Cross then?' grinned the cab driver, displaying a half set of blackened teeth.

'Yes, I suppose there is nothing else for it,' Ravenscroft sighed. 'Stop off at the telegraph office, if you will. We must let our wives know that we will not be home tonight or we shall be in serious trouble, Tom.'

* * *

A few minutes later, Ravenscroft and Crabb alighted from the cab outside the Black Cross.

'Come back for us at eight in the morning,' Ravenscroft instructed the old cabman.

'I reckons that all depends on the weather.'

'We will make it well worth your while.'

'Right you are. Good night. Sleep well; watch out for strangers in the night,' laughed Judd loudly, before cracking his whip and speeding off down the road.

'Ah well, if it is not Inspector Ravenscroft again.' Symonds smiled like an old friend as the two detectives entered the Black Cross.

'It seems that Sergeant Crabb and I are unable to leave the town tonight due to the inclement weather, and consequently we have need of two rooms for the night, if you please,' said Ravenscroft.

'Well now, I will see what we can do,' replied the landlord, shaking his head as he looked down at the ledger. 'Now then that might be very difficult, very difficult indeed.'

'You had rooms available this morning. Surely you cannot have many people dropping in without notice, in such weather?' asked Ravenscroft.

'That's as may be, but we always like to keep some rooms available for those unexpected travellers who might arrive at such a late hour.'

'We are such travellers,' Ravenscroft persisted.

'Ah, that you are indeed; I will see what I can do for you. Now, come to think of it, I do believe that we may have two such rooms available. Rooms 2 and 3 are at your disposal.'

'We will take them. Wasn't it Room 2 where the late Mr Conningsby was boarded?'

'That it was indeed, but you will find that all traces of that poor unfortunate gentleman's residence there have now been removed.'

'I don't mind taking that room,' offered Crabb.

'Thank you, Tom, but that will not be necessary. We will take possession now, if we may. Two plates of your finest supper and ale in thirty minutes would be most acceptable.'

'I will be having a word with the wife to see if we can accommodate your good selves.'

* * *

'Well, Tom, this is turning into a strange case.' Ravenscroft laid down his knife and fork on the empty plate, as he and Crabb sat later in the snug of the Black Cross. 'We first came here endeavouring to discover who had murdered old Mr Stebbins, and soon discovered the moneylending activities of the old bookseller. His book gave us the names of Sir John Critchwood and Peter Nightingale, amongst many others in the town. Both these men are involved in the Bromsgrove Gas Light and Coke Company. Sir John borrowed two hundred and fifty pounds from Stebbins, so that he could buy up land in Charford, where he intends to build nearly a hundred houses and no doubt make a tidy profit on the deal.'

'The houses of which would also be supplied with electricity and coke from Sir John's company,' interrupted Crabb.

'Indeed. Then we discovered that poor man's body on the railway line, and the letter found in his old Bible asking him to come to the town. If only we could find out who had sent him the letter, and why he had been told to visit here. Who was this Eustace Conningsby? It is a pity that his effects do not tell us anything more about him. He does not appear to have been a local man, and neither Troth nor Sir John say they recognise the name. Yet I am sure that he was known to Mary Nightingale.'

'Mr Fitzwilliam at the bank thought he may have heard of Conningsby.'

'Yes, but even he could not place the name.'

'What about the letter?'

Ravenscroft took the folded paper from his coat pocket and again read its contents. 'It states quite clearly here that Conningsby is to travel to Bromsgrove, to meet up with the writer, who has "the required document in my possession." What document was that? Did our murderer kill Conningsby to prevent him from obtaining that document? This is all very frustrating, Tom, but I know that whatever tomorrow brings we must endeavour to get out of this town at all costs and return home for Christmas, even if we have to dig our way across to Ledbury.'

'I know that Mrs Crabb and the children will not be too pleased if I am not there with them to enjoy the Christmas dinner,' added Crabb.

'Let us have a look at old Mr Stebbins's account book once again,' suggested Ravenscroft, taking out the old battered volume from his coat pocket. 'There are certainly plenty of names here. It appears that half the citizens of Bromsgrove must have borrowed money from the old bookseller at one time or another, including Detective Inspector Bullman, although I must admit that five pounds does not seem to be a large amount in his case. Nevertheless, we must ask him about it when we can find a convenient time. Good Lord!'

'What is it, sir?' asked a startled Crabb.

'Look at the handwriting in this book. Now look again at the letter sent to Conningsby. What do you notice?' Ravenscroft laid out the two documents on the table.

Crabb studied the two items. 'They are written in the same hand.'

'Exactly! See the similarities, particularly in the capital letters and the way the "q" in particular is written with that embellishment on the end of the tail. So it was old Stebbins who wrote this letter to Conningsby! How foolish we were not to have noticed it sooner. Two days after this letter was sent to Conningsby, the bookseller was dead.'

'Which means that whoever killed him must have also murdered Conningsby?'

'Yes, but the question is why? Of course, in the letter Mr Stebbins was telling Conningsby to meet him here in Bromsgrove, when he would show him an important document. When he arrived here however, Conningsby discovered the bookseller was already dead. That must have been quite a shock to him. I wonder what that document was all about. It must have been quite valuable and important to have brought Conningsby here, but whatever it was, it cost two men their lives.'

'It could still be amongst old Mr Stebbins's papers?' suggested Crabb.

'That makes it all the more imperative that we go back to the shop tonight, and make a thorough search for this document.' Ravenscroft rose quickly from his seat. 'Fortunately we still have the key. But first I must instruct our landlord to stoke up the fire in my bedroom. I have never known such a cold and draughty place in all my life.'

* * *

As Ravenscroft and Crabb made their way along the high street, they saw a familiar figure coming towards them with a basket on her arm, wrapped up warm against the cold.

'Good evening to you, Mrs Marquis,' said Ravenscroft, raising his hat.

'Who is that? Why, yes, it is Inspector Ravenscroft if I am not mistaken.'

'You are out rather late, it being such a bad night,' smiled Ravenscroft.

'I am just on my way to drop off some provisions for an old friend of mine who is housebound. With this snow falling so steadily, I am not sure if the grocer will be able to deliver to her tomorrow. I hope your investigation is going well, Inspector.'

'As well as can be expected, I thank you. Tell me Mrs Marquis, do you know how long Mr Stebbins had resided at the bookshop?' asked Ravenscroft.

'Oh, a very long time, I should think. He was already living there when Mr Marquis and I moved into the courtyard and opened our little shop.'

'And when was that?'

'Twenty-two years ago, come next February. We opened on St Valentine's Day,' nodded the old woman, a distant look in her eyes. 'It was all so long ago.'

'I suppose a lot of people used to visit the bookshop?'

'Yes, there were always people coming and going.'

'Thank you, Mrs Marquis. If we don't see you again, both my colleague and I wish you a pleasant and gentle Christmas.'

'That is very kind of you, Inspector. I shall be spending Christmas alone, as I did last year, although I will try and read *A Christmas Carol*, as I have done for these past five years. Have you read it, Inspector?'

'I had that pleasure a few years ago,' replied Ravenscroft.

'There is something quite satisfying about the book — an old miser who sees the error of his ways, and is saved for us all on Christmas morning. It shows that even a sinner can obtain redemption, if he is prepared to let goodness into his soul. I suppose there is hope and salvation for us all. But I am rambling. You must forgive me. I must not detain you. I suppose you two have families to welcome you home?'

'We do indeed.'

'You have left it rather late to get home for Christmas. The roads out of the town must be quite bad.'

'Yes, but we have found rooms at the Black Cross, and I hope the weather will be better tomorrow to enable us to return home for Christmas.'

'Then I wish you well, and all good success with your endeavours,' smiled Mrs Marquis.

'A nice woman,' remarked Crabb. 'She must find it lonely at Christmas.'

'Indeed, we must be thankful that we have loved ones awaiting our return. Right, Tom, let us quicken our pace. The sooner we get out of this snow and cold wind, the better.'

'Spare a penny for an old man,' called out a voice as the two detectives turned off the main street and into the passageway that led into the courtyard.

'Jonas, is it not?' asked Ravenscroft looking down at the bundle of rags and the outstretched hand.

'Bless you, sir, you gave me a coin yesterday,' replied the old beggar staring up at the detective.

'It is very cold to be out here tonight. Have you nowhere to go?' said Ravenscroft, looking into the man's darkened, sunken eyes.

'It costs sixpence for a bed at Murphys.'

'What is Murphys?' asked Crabb.

'Lodging house.' The man spoke in barely a whisper.

'Well here is a shilling, for tonight and for Christmas. Get yourself a warm bed,' said Ravenscroft.

'And a warm meal.' Crabb handed over another coin.

'God bless you. Thank goodness for Christian souls.' Jonas rose to his feet, and walked quickly out into the main street.

'Poor man,' said Crabb.

'Yes. Makes you wonder what could have happened to a person like that, to have left him now in such reduced circumstances. We must thank our blessings that we took the right path when it was offered to us.'

As Crabb and Ravenscroft made their way into the courtyard, all that could be heard was the sound of their boots on the snow-covered cobbles. A fragile gas lamp threw out its faltering rays across the white snow and flickered on the narrow bull's-eye windows of the bookshop.

'Lock the door behind us, Tom,' instructed Ravenscroft after he and Crabb had made their way into the building. 'We don't want to be disturbed. Now, I think I remember that there are candles still in one or two of the candlesticks. And here are some safety matches on this shelf.' He lit the two candles. 'That is better. Now, where do we start?' pondered Ravenscroft.

'We have already looked upstairs and there was nothing there.'

'Then whatever we are looking for must still be down here. If you were old Mr Stebbins, and you were in possession of a valuable document which you did not want to be discovered, where would you hide it?'

'Inside one of the books?' suggested Crabb.

'That is a good suggestion. You take that candle and examine the bookshelves on that side of the room. I'll take the other one and look on the other shelves. I am afraid we need to take out each volume and see if there are any documents secreted between the pages. It could be quite a laborious occupation, but one that we need to undertake.'

For the next thirty minutes the two men busied themselves in searching through the rows of books.

'Nothing on these shelves.' Crabb sounded disappointed.

'Nothing here either. Come over here, Tom. Do you notice anything unusual about the books on this shelf?'

'There is a space there, between those two books.'

'Do you see who is the author of the books on either side of the missing space.'

'Anthony Trollope.'

'Exactly! Do you remember that Peter Nightingale telling us that the reason for his visit to the bookseller was that the old man had found a particular book by Anthony Trollope, which he was anxious to add to his own collection?'

'*The Last Chronicle of Barset*.'

'Yes, and that title may well have been the missing volume in this collection of books by Trollope. Nightingale must have stolen it when he was here that day.'

'Could it have contained the missing document?'

'I don't know. Let us search the back office again. That was where old Mr Stebbins was killed. What on earth!' exclaimed Ravenscroft shading his eyes from the bright light that suddenly shone into the room.

'It's someone outside,' said Crabb.

'Open up!' shouted a loud voice.

'You had better unlock the door, Tom.'

Crabb turned the key, and the figure holding the lantern stepped quickly into the shop.

'Now then, stay where you are. You are under arrest. You have no right to be here. Now, come quietly. Why, bless my soul, if it isn't Inspector Ravenscroft and Sergeant Crabb.'

'Constable Roberts, if you could stop shining that light directly into my eyes, I would be obliged,' said Ravenscroft.

'Sorry, sir, I did not know that you would be here. I was just undertaking my nightly patrol, when I happened to see a light coming from inside,' replied Roberts apologetically.

'That's alright, Constable. We have been forced to stay in the town for the night, at the Black Cross, due to the inclement weather, so Sergeant Crabb and I thought we would make another search of the old bookseller's effects.'

'Of course, sir. I will be on my way. Sorry to have disturbed you.'

'That is alright, Constable. You have been most diligent in your duty, which is to be commended.'

'Good of you to say so. Good night,' replied Roberts, making his way out of the shop.

Crabb again secured the door.

'Now for the back room,' said Ravenscroft. 'Stop, Tom! Do you notice anything different in this room since we were here yesterday?'

'Yes, that pile of folders on the floor. I am sure that they were in a neat tidy pile when we were here. Now they look as though they have been disturbed,' answered Crabb.

'My thought exactly. Someone has been here since our last visit, and has made a search through these folders. I wonder if they were after the same document that we are looking for.'

'That is rather a blow.'

'They may not have found what they were seeking. There is nothing else for it, we shall have to go through the lot of them.' Ravenscroft took up nearly half of the pile, and placed them on the old bookseller's desk.

'What exactly are we looking for?' asked Crabb.

'I don't really know. Perhaps we will know that when we see it. It must be a document that Stebbins valued, and which he also considered would have been of importance to Eustace Conningsby. I see that the old man has written in pencil on the outside of each folder. This first one says "Map of Old Bromsgrove", the next one appears to be an old will and inventory for someone called Hamment of Long Crendon in Oxfordshire, the next an old auction poster for the sale of a farm near Ombersley . . .'

For the next few minutes, the two men continued to work their way through the various folders.

'There is nothing here of value that I can see is of relevance to this case. Bring the rest over, Tom, if you will.'

'Yes, sir.'

'Now what do we have here? More old wills, maps, newspapers, posters, and so forth. I see that this folder is empty.'

'Is there any writing on the outside?' asked Crabb.

'Yes, look there, Tom.' Ravenscroft pointed to the letters. '"Critchwood and Conningsby." My word! I think we have found what we were looking for. But it is a pity that someone else has got here before us.'

'It must have contained something of importance for it to have been stolen.'

'Yes. Fortunately for us, whoever took what was inside this folder either failed to notice the rather faded pencil lettering on the outside, or considered it of little value and was happy to discard it here.'

'So the old bookseller was in possession of a document, which he considered to be of value to Eustace Conningsby,' said Crabb.

'Furthermore we now know that the document also had something to do with Sir John Critchwood, and in all probability whoever killed the bookseller also wanted to get his or her hands on this document. Then the murderer also did away with Eustace Conningsby to prevent him from finding it. The question now is, what exactly was in this document that it was worth killing two men for?'

CHAPTER SIX

BROMSGROVE, 24 DECEMBER

The church clock had struck twelve before Ravenscroft and Crabb returned to the Black Cross. Finding the bar empty of all persons, they helped themselves to a nightcap and a welcoming seat before the warming fire, before retiring for the night.

Ravenscroft, after bidding Crabb farewell, opened the door of Room 2. Despite the fire still burning in the grate, he nevertheless found the room cold and uninviting, and decided he would remove only his outer coat, before climbing into the bed and pulling the covers closely up to his chin.

As he lay back and looked up at the ceiling, the light from the solitary candle flickering gently in the draughty room, Ravenscroft went over the events of the previous three days, from the time when he had received Maisie Stebbins's letter, to the finding of the dead man Eustace Conningsby on the railway line. Then there had been the discovery of the missing folder, which seemed not only to link together both Conningsby and Sir John, but also to unite the two investigations into the deaths of old Mr Stebbins and the dead man on the track. What precisely was the document that had brought Conningsby to the town of Bromsgrove, and ultimately to his brutal death? Could it have been anything to do with the land at Charford that Sir John was so desperate to acquire for his proposed housing development, and if so, what had it to do with Conningsby? What part did Peter and Mary Nightingale have to play in all this, and had the farmer, Troth, perhaps resorted to drastic measures to secure his property? It was all very perplexing and Ravenscroft realised that he was powerless, at present, to draw any conclusions from the evidence he and Crabb had unearthed. He decided he would journey over to Bournheath, as soon as daylight broke, and confront Sir John with his findings. The landowner had denied ever knowing Conningsby, but Ravenscroft was sure that he had been lying, and now that faded writing on the outside of the file seemed to confirm the relationship between the two men.

A sudden breeze caused the candle to flutter wildly, making the shadows that it threw on to the walls seem even larger and more disturbing. Ravenscroft realised that despite his clothing and the bedclothes he still felt cold and unsettled. Rising quickly from his bed, he strode over to the dying fire and sought to revive the spluttering flames by adding the remaining meagre two pieces of coal from the scuttle. Then as he turned to retrace his steps back towards the bed, a cold wind blew across his face with such force that the solitary candle on the bedside table was suddenly extinguished. Ravenscroft paused, attempting to adjust his eyes to the darkness in the room. Then he noticed that the draught had also dampened the fire, leaving only a solitary red glow from beneath one of the coals.

Reaching into his pocket, he was relieved to find his hand closing on the box of safety matches from the bookseller's. Stretching forth his arm, Ravenscroft inched his way slowly back towards the bed. After nearly colliding with the bedpost at the foot, he reached out towards the bedside table and ran his fingers over the candlestick. Removing the box of matches from his pocket, he took out one and struck it along the side of the box, and was rewarded by a welcoming spark, but as he sought to bring the flame towards the wick of the candle, it died before his eyes.

Taking another match, he repeated the action, but the feeble spark went the same way as the first, and although he tried a further two times each of his efforts met with the same fate. The box now empty, and the fire almost completely extinguished, Ravenscroft decided that he could do no more, and clambered back into the bed, where he again drew the bedcover closely around him, before closing his eyes in an attempt to remove all thought of the inhospitable room from his mind.

As he felt his eyes becoming heavy, he saw before him the railway track, the dead man lying on the rails, the blood seeming to splatter on to the cold white snow. He shivered at the memory. Then he saw himself again in old Mr Stebbins's room surrounded by large piles of musty old books where the air was damp and claustrophobic. He saw his hand reaching out for one of the books, but then he heard the sound of laughter and looked up to see one of the bookcases suddenly falling downwards towards him and knowing that he could do little to prevent being engulfed by its contents.

'Ravenscroft! Ravenscroft!'

Ravenscroft woke with a start. He sat bolt upright in bed and stared out into the darkness. He realised that he must have drifted off to sleep, but now something, or someone, had called out his name and had caused him to waken. He touched his clammy forehead. Despite the intense cold of the bedroom he was perspiring beneath his clothes.

Then he suddenly became aware of a strange shape drifting slowly across one of the walls.

'Who is there?' Ravenscroft called out, in a voice that seemed unlike his own. 'Crabb, is that you?'

There was no response.

'I know you are there. Show yourself, man,' demanded Ravenscroft in voice that was scarcely bolder than before. 'Who are you?'

A sudden noise made him turn, and he saw that the fire in the grate had quickly sprung into life. Grabbing the candlestick, he dashed over towards the hearth and quickly lit the wick. Then turning around he held the light above his head and moved it slowly from one side of the room to the other, trying to see if anyone was lingering in the darkness.

'No one,' said Ravenscroft.

He made his way back to the bed, protecting the flame with the side of his hand.

'Stupid imagination!' he muttered as he climbed into the bed, after first placing the candlestick back on the side table.

'Sleep,' Ravenscroft sighed, as he turned his face towards the flickering flame.

* * *

Ravenscroft awoke as the first signs of daybreak were inching their way between the panes of glass in the bedroom window. He reached out for his pocket watch and saw that the time was a few minutes past eight.

Cursing himself for his lateness, he walked over to the side table and poured some of the icy water into the bowl, before splashing the liquid on to his face.

A few minutes later, Ravenscroft made his way down to the bar of the Black Cross, where he saw that Crabb was sitting before a roaring fire.

'Good morning, Tom, I trust you slept well?' asked Ravenscroft, walking over to the fire and warming his cold hands in front of the flames.

'Very well, thank you; and you?' answered Crabb.

'To tell the truth, I have never spent a more uncomfortable night in my whole life. It was so cold and draughty, the bed was uneven and lumpy, and when I finally fell asleep I found myself being woken up by a strange noise. I thought there was someone in the room in the middle of the night. It, whatever it was, called out my name, and I am sure I saw a shadow crossing along one of the walls.'

'Ah, that will be the old cavalier,' interjected Symonds, suddenly appearing from behind the corner.

'The cavalier?' asked Ravenscroft.

'One of the royalists who was killed in the Civil War, but to be sure he is harmless enough. On the other hand, it could be the young servant girl who was murdered here.'

'Oh, when was that?' asked Ravenscroft his curiosity aroused.

'Many years ago, long before either you or I were born, Inspector, so you don't need to trouble yourself with trying to find out who committed the ghastly deed,' said Symonds in a cheery manner.

'Thank goodness for that. We have enough to be going on with at the present, without trying to find out who murdered a poor servant girl,' said Ravenscroft.

'There again, it could have been one of those prisoners who were hanged out the back of the premises.'

'What prisoners?'

'Ah, well, you see, they do say that in the olden days convicted criminals spent the night in the cellars beneath the inn, before they were led out the next morning for their execution. But they won't do you any harm either, if you speak to them in a kindly manner, that is.'

'This must be the most haunted place in the whole country,' muttered a sceptical Crabb.

'How many more ghosts do you have?' asked Ravenscroft.

'That is all that I have seen. Although there have also been strange goings-on in the kitchen, from time to time,' said the landlord, warming to his narrative.

'I'm sure there have been,' interrupted Ravenscroft. 'But right now I would be grateful if you could serve us some breakfast, as soon as possible.'

'Oh to be sure, that I will,' replied Symonds, before making his way out towards the back room.

'Civil War royalists, young girl murdered, prisoners executed in the back yard — I have never heard of such nonsense,' said Crabb. 'Our host has a very vivid imagination.'

'I'm inclined to agree with you, Tom. I have never believed in ghosts. It's those villains who are still alive that cause all the trouble. I was sure that there was someone, or something in my room last night, but I suppose the dark and cold can play havoc with one's imagination. Anyway, enough of all that. Have you had any more thoughts about this case?'

'Only that I am inclined to believe that the answer lies with Sir John Critchwood,' replied Crabb. 'His name, together with that of Conningsby, was written on old Mr Stebbins's folder, and in all probability it was Sir John, or one of his men, who stole its contents after killing the bookseller, to prevent Conningsby obtaining it.'

'My thoughts exactly, Tom, but we don't know that Sir John actually killed old Mr Stebbins. It could be that someone else killed both Conningsby and Stebbins. Interestingly, the murderer did not search for the documents at the time of the killing, but appears to have returned much later. On our first visit the folders were all neatly stacked up in the corner of the room.'

'Why did he not take them at the time?' asked Crabb.

'There cannot have been enough time for him to have undertaken the search. When he had killed the bookseller, the killer was anxious to put distance between himself and the scene of the crime. He knew he could return much later and search for the missing papers at his leisure and when he knew that he would not be disturbed.'

'He seems to have waited a long time. Old Mr Stebbins has been dead for nearly a week and a half.'

'Yes, that is what worries me, unless of course it was Conningsby who took the papers!' exclaimed Ravenscroft. 'When we first arrived here two days ago Conningsby had not long been in town. He must have learnt of the bookseller's death, and came out here in the evening, after we had visited earlier in the day, and searched for the missing papers.'

'But the papers were not on his person or amongst his possessions in his room here at the inn.'

'That was because whoever killed Conningsby made sure that they also took the papers before depositing the body on the railway line. That would mean that whoever killed Stebbins must have also waited until Conningsby showed up, so that he could then kill him as well. The question is, why were the contents of that file so important to our killer?'

'So we will confront Sir John this morning.'

'Indeed we will. I am sure that Sir John knew of Conningsby, and I mean to get at the truth at all costs . . . but I see that our landlord has returned with our breakfast.'

'That I have, indeed.' Symonds placed two plates of food on the table.

'Those eggs look remarkably good,' commented Ravenscroft.

'Oh, they are. Laid this morning, they were, by our own fine hens out the back.'

'Please thank your wife,' said Ravenscroft.

'Would that I could. She is away visiting her family for Christmas, sighed Symmonds.'

'What is the weather like today? Have you been outside to see?' asked Ravenscroft, eagerly picking up his knife and fork.

'Well now, maybe I have been outside, but then maybe I haven't.'

'Have you, or have you not, been outside this morning, and if you have, could you possibly enlighten us as to the state of the roads.' Ravenscroft almost wished that he had not bothered to ask the question in the first place.

'What I meant was that no, I have not been out to see what state the roads are in, but yes I have been outside to the stables, to feed the horse,' replied Symonds, wiping his hands on his greasy apron.

'Is there snow on the grounds, yes or no, and if so, how deep is it?' asked an exasperated Ravenscroft.

'Well now, I would say that there is enough snow on the ground to make it most difficult to walk, but not enough snow that a horse would not be able to get through it with a little encouragement from your good selves,' smiled the landlord.

'Thank you,' said Ravenscroft before bringing a forkful of food to his mouth.

'I'll just get that coffee for you.'

'We would be obliged.'

Ravenscroft and Crabb continued with their breakfasts.

'That was incredibly good.' Ravenscroft returned his knife and fork to his plate. 'This place may be cold and draughty, and its former occupants of a dubious nature, but at least the cook makes a tolerable breakfast. Now we will see if old Judd is waiting for us outside. After we have been to Bournheath and confronted Sir John, I hope we will be able to conclude this case. But whatever we do today it is important that we both leave this town by the middle of the afternoon, to be sure of returning home for Christmas. We can only pray that the trains are operating again. Mrs Ravenscroft will never forgive me if I am not there tomorrow to carve the goose.'

'I know that my Jennie would never speak to me again,' added Crabb.

Both men looked up as the door of the room to the bar was suddenly flung open, and a breathless Constable Roberts rushed forwards. 'Thank goodness you are still here!'

'Whatever is the matter?'

'It's Sir John Critchwood. Terrible news! He's been shot!'

CHAPTER SEVEN

BOURNHEATH

'What do you mean he has been shot?' asked Ravenscroft, rising quickly from his chair.

'Apparently he locked himself in his study last night, and shot himself,' replied the anxious policeman.

'Good Lord!' exclaimed Crabb.

'One of the servants has just come over to the police station with the news,' continued Roberts.

'Where is Inspector Bullman?' said Ravenscroft.

'Still at court in Worcester. That's why I came straight across to you, sir. I remember you saying last night that you were staying here.'

'You did right, Roberts. We had better get over there as fast as we can.'

'I've got the trap outside.'

'Good man.'

The three policemen rushed out of the inn.

Ravenscroft noticed a cab across the road. 'I see that old Judd is waiting for us. We had better tell him that his services will not be required.'

'Good morning to you, governor,' said Judd, raising his cap.

'I am afraid that we do not want your cab at the present time as Constable Roberts has the police trap waiting for us. Here is a coin for your trouble.' Ravenscroft passed over the money.

'Thanking you kindly. I'll be seeing you again. I'll be back before I come,' said Judd.

Ravenscroft smiled at this strange utterance.

* * *

As the trap drew up outside Old Dodford Manor, Ravenscroft observed that March, Sir John's land agent, and Travers the footman were waiting anxiously for their arrival.

'Inspector,' said March sternly, coming forward to meet the three policemen.

'We came as soon as we heard the news,' said Ravenscroft.

'Doctor Fortescue is with the body now.'

'Then you had best lead on, March,' urged Ravenscroft.

The policemen followed March and Travers through the hall, up the grand staircase and along a corridor on the first floor, until they reached a room at the end.

'This is Sir John's study,' said March.

'I thought that was on the ground floor, when I visited Sir John yesterday,' said Ravenscroft.

'The room on the ground floor is where he conducts most of his business during the day. This is where he prefers to work alone in the evenings,' replied March, before opening the door.

Ravenscroft, Crabb and Roberts entered a small wood-panelled room, where a portly man came forward to meet them. 'I am Doctor Fortescue. You must be the police?'

'Yes. I am Detective Inspector Ravenscroft, and these are my associates, Detective Sergeant Crabb and Constable Roberts.'

'I thought Inspector Bullman was in charge at Bromsgrove Police Station?'

'The inspector has been called away to appear at court in Worcester.'

'Well as you can see, Inspector, it is not a pretty state of affairs, but then suicide is never pleasant.' The doctor stood aside so that Ravenscroft could see the figure of the dead man slumped in his armchair.

'What makes you think it was suicide?'

'He appears to have shot himself through the left temple, which caused him to drop the gun on the floor as he sank back into the chair,' answered Fortescue.

'He locked the door behind him,' added Travers. 'Mr March broke it open when we could not raise an answer from him.'

'I see. When do you think this took place, Doctor?' asked Ravenscroft kneeling down and looking up into the dead man's blood-stained face.

'I would say that he has been dead for over twelve hours. He must have killed himself shortly after saying good evening to us all.'

'Twelve hours! Did nobody hear the shot? Forgive me, Doctor Fortescue, but you were here yesterday evening?'

'Yes. Sir John was holding a small dinner party yesterday evening, and as the hour was late and many of the roads impassable because of the snow, we were all invited to stay for the night.'

'What time did Sir John retire for the evening?'

'At ten o'clock.'

'You say that Sir John liked to work in this room late in the evening.' Ravenscroft addressed the land agent. 'Was he in the habit of doing this every night?'

'Yes,' said March. 'He liked to work alone up here.'

'Did Sir John receive any visitors yesterday evening after he retired to this room?'

'No,' said Travers. 'The dinner guests didn't trouble him, and there were no other visitors to the house.'

'And did he always lock the door?'

'Not usually,' said Travers.

'How long did he usually work in here, before retiring for the night?'

'For one or two hours, I believe. His bedroom is next door.'

'He sleeps separately from Lady Critchwood?'

'Yes. She has the adjoining room but one.'

'And what is the room between?'

'Lady Critchwood's dressing room.'

'Thank you. How was the body discovered this morning?' asked Ravenscroft as Crabb made notes in his pocketbook.

'We all came down to breakfast at eight. Sir John was not there,' said Fortescue.

'Was it Sir John's usual custom to welcome guests at breakfast?' interjected Ravenscroft.

'Yes, sir,' replied Travers.

'So what happened when Sir John did not appear?'

'Lady Critchwood thought that perhaps her husband was ill, and so I was sent to knock on his bedroom door,' replied the footman.

'Go on,' urged Ravenscroft.

'When I received no reply, I entered the bedroom. I could see that Sir John had not slept in his bed last night, so I assumed that perhaps he had been taken ill in his study. However when I went to open the door I found that it was locked. I knocked several times, and called out, and upon receiving no reply I went straight to find Mr March here, in his office.'

'Mr March perhaps you would be kind enough to continue the narrative?' asked Ravenscroft.

'Yes. Travers and I came back to the room. The door was locked. I called out, but there was no reply. I put my shoulder to the door, and we forced our way into the room. I made a brief examination of Sir John, but it was obvious that he was dead. I then went downstairs to inform Lady Critchwood and to ask Doctor Fortescue to come up, while instructing Travers here to send the coachman as quickly as possible to the police station.'

'Thank you, gentlemen.' Ravenscroft knelt down and picked up the gun from the floor. 'A single-chamber revolver, which has certainly been fired. Can either of you identify this weapon?'

'It belongs to Sir John. He usually kept it in the desk drawer over there,' answered Travers.

'If we assume that Sir John locked the door, then where is the key?' asked Ravenscroft.

'It is not in the keyhole.' Crabb was examining the door. 'Ah, here it is, on the floor.'

'It must have dropped out when we forced the door open,' said March.

'Doctor Fortescue, who else was present at dinner last night?'

'There was Lady Critchwood and her son, Christopher. Then there was Mr Lowbeam and the French gentleman, Monsieur Hubert.'

'Forgive my interruption, but who are these gentlemen?' asked Ravenscroft, as Crabb wrote the names down in his pocketbook.

'Mr Lowbeam is the family solicitor. I have never met the French gentleman before, but I believe that he was a recent acquaintance of Sir John. Then there was Mr Peter Nightingale and his sister. That is all.'

'Mr Nightingale? That is most interesting. Well, thank you, gentlemen. I would be obliged if you could leave us to examine the dead man and the room. Constable Roberts, would you go downstairs and make sure no one leaves the house? Ask the guests and family to gather in the drawing room in fifteen minutes, as I would like to speak with them all.'

'Yes, sir.'

'If you will excuse me, I will make arrangements to remove the body,' said Fortescue.

'Very well. How long has Sir John been your patient?'

'It must be for over thirty years now.'

'Can any of you think why Sir John would have taken his own life?' asked Ravenscroft.

'I am not quite sure what you mean,' asked a bewildered March.

'Was his mood low? Was he unduly worried or concerned about financial matters? Did he say that he was going to end his life?' prompted Ravenscroft.

'No, sir. There was nothing like that,' answered Travers.

'Was he suffering from any kind of illness, Doctor?'

'No. Sir John was in perfect health, considering his age, and his riding accident.'

'What riding accident?'

'Sir John fell from his horse while out hunting some five or six years ago. He broke his collar bone and injured his shoulder, but he made a good recovery.'

'He never complained that this old injury was causing him pain?' continued Ravenscroft.

'No. If he was in pain, he never confided in me.'

After the three men had left the room, Ravenscroft turned to his sergeant. 'Close the door, Tom. We don't want to be disturbed.'

Ravenscroft studied the scene for a few moments, before reaching into the pockets of the dead man's smoking jacket. 'There is nothing of interest here. Check the window and see if anyone could have left the room that way.'

Crabb walked over to the window. 'Window is bolted and locked from the inside. It looks like quite a formidable drop to the ground anyway.'

'So whoever killed Sir John did not leave that way.'

'You don't believe it was suicide, then?' asked Crabb.

'No. What do you think, Tom?'

'It seems most unlikely, especially as no one has said that his mind was addled.'

'Precisely! If you were going to kill yourself, why would you go to the bother of locking yourself in the room while you did so?'

'So you would not be disturbed?' suggested Crabb.

'Perhaps, but here is another interesting point. When we met with Sir John yesterday, I am sure that he was writing with his right hand. If you were right-handed and you raised the gun to your head like this, the bullet would have gone through the right temple. Sir John, however, appears to have been shot through the left temple.'

'So someone else shot him?'

'It would appear that way. However, we have to remember that the door was locked. How could anyone have locked the door from the inside, and then made their escape from this room? Only ghosts are said to walk through solid walls.' Ravenscroft removed his spectacles and rubbed them gently on his handkerchief as he thought out loud. 'I doubt if anyone would have heard the shot, as this appears to be in a remote part of the house. The room is also covered with this thick panelling, which must have deadened the sound of the shot. That is why nobody would hear it.'

'How could the killer have escaped?' asked Crabb, perplexed.

'By locking the door behind him, as he left, from the outside.'

'But the key was inside the room when we found it.'

'Yes, so that only leaves two possibilities. Either the door was unlocked at the time of the killing, and March and Travers forced the door merely to give themselves an alibi. Or someone else committed the murder, locked the door behind them, and when they entered the room this morning to view the body, dropped the key on the floor over there by the door, while everyone else was distracted.'

'Why would either March or Travers want to kill their master?'

'Money or hatred are the obvious motives. We need to know who exactly entered this room after March and Travers had broken in. I want to know the exact movements of everyone in the house, from ten o'clock yesterday evening when Sir John bade his guests good night, until when his body was discovered this morning.'

'It is interesting that two of those guests are Peter and Mary Nightingale,' observed Crabb.

'Yes, it is strange how this investigation keeps coming back to that pair.'

'What has Sir John's death to do with the murders of Mr Stebbins and Eustace Conningsby?'

'At this present time I cannot answer that question, but remember that we were coming here today to confront Sir John about his connections to Conningsby, and to enquire about his business interest in that land at Charford. Unfortunately someone got here before us.'

'So are we now looking for the same killer who murdered all three men?'

'It looks very much that way. Let us examine Sir John's papers on the desk over there. We probably won't find Mr Stebbins's missing documents — whoever killed Sir John would not have left empty-handed — but we dare not leave any stone unturned.'

For the next few minutes, the two men went through the papers on Sir John's desk, and then turned their attention to the rows of books on the shelves that lined the room.

'It is as I feared. If Sir John was in possession of the missing papers then they have certainly been taken. His papers seem to relate to various jottings from some of the books in his collection, mainly notes on natural history and horses. What do you deduce from Sir John's book collection?'

'That his interests were the same — sporting, farming and natural history.'

'Indeed. Note that there are no poems, novels, or works on theology or philosophy. I think we can safely conclude that Sir John's interests were of the here and now, rather than romantic.'

'Not the kind of man who would want to kill himself?'

'Perhaps. It is time we spoke with the people in this house. I think we will not disclose any of our suspicions at this point, but it may do no harm to admit our concerns. Of course, we may be drawing the wrong conclusions from all of this.'

'What do you mean?'

'It is possible that Sir John was feeling unwell and that he decided to commit suicide, locking the door behind him, killing himself using his left hand, and that the key fell out of the lock when the door was forced open this morning.'

'But you don't really believe that.'

'No. I suspect foul play. Furthermore, I think that whoever killed Sir John must still be in this house. Whoever murdered him most probably also killed Mr Stebbins and Eustace Conningsby, and all for a piece of paper. The question is, who killed them all, and for what purpose?'

* * *

Doctor Fortescue met Ravenscroft and Crabb as they entered the drawing room.

'There you are, Ravenscroft. We were wondering where the devil you had got to. Never mind, you are here now. May I introduce Lady Critchwood? This is Inspector Ravenscroft.'

'Lady Critchwood, please accept my condolences upon the death of your husband,' said Ravenscroft, coming forward to meet the upright woman, with an ashen face and worn complexion, who sat at the nearest end of the sofa. 'It is a very sad business.'

The woman said nothing, as Ravenscroft looked up at the young man standing behind his mother.

'I believe you know Mr Critchwood,' continued Fortescue.

'Indeed,' replied Ravenscroft, as the young man fidgeted nervously with his pocket watch.

'This is Mr Nightingale and his sister Miss Mary Nightingale.'

'We have met already,' smiled Ravenscroft.

'This gentleman is Mr Lowbeam.' He indicated a tweed-clad, middle-aged man.

'Mr Lowbeam, I understand that you are the family solicitor?'

'That is so, Inspector.'

'And this gentleman is Monsieur Hubert,' said Fortescue, referring to the immaculately dressed, moustached man, who had been looking out of the window when Ravenscroft had entered the room.

'Ladies and gentlemen,' began Ravenscroft, aware that all eyes were upon him, 'my name is Detective Inspector Ravenscroft. Inspector Bullman of the local constabulary is at present at court in Worcester, so Sergeant Crabb and I will be carrying out enquiries in his absence. I am given to understand that you were all present in the house yesterday evening when Sir John went upstairs to his study.'

'That is so,' answered Fortescue.

'I presume that none of you saw Sir John again?'

One or two of the company nodded their agreement, as Hubert returned to staring out of the window.

'I have examined both the body of Sir John, and the contents of his study, and I have to tell you that I am not entirely satisfied that Sir John took his own life.'

'That is nonsense, man,' interjected Lowbeam. 'You saw for yourself that Sir John had locked the door of the room behind him when he retired. No one could have entered and left the room afterwards.'

'We had to break it down this morning,' added March.

'Indeed, but there are certain inconsistencies,' Ravenscroft began.

'Inconsistences!' interrupted Fortescue. 'I examined the body myself. It is obvious to anyone that Sir John took his own life.'

'That may be so Doctor Fortescue, but I would be failing in my duty if I did not examine all possibilities in this case. There are a great number of questions that need to be answered. Consequently, it is important that no one leaves the house this morning until I have interviewed each one of you individually.'

'Look, Inspector,' said Fortescue coming closer to the detective, placing his hand on his shoulder, and speaking in a lower key, 'you can see how Lady Critchwood and her son are distressed by this whole business. It won't do any good to prolong the affair. Have a heart.'

'I am sorry, Doctor Fortescue, but I have to prepare a report for my superiors. It is important that the facts are recorded as close to the time of the crime as possible. Now if I may have access to the study down here, I will call you in one at a time if may. I can assure you that I will be as quick as I can, and given the time of year we will not detain you for more than is absolutely necessary,' said Ravenscroft politely but firmly.

'Very well,' Fortescue sighed. 'But I have patients to see.'

'Then perhaps we might start with you, Doctor.'

'And I have an urgent meeting to attend at midday,' shouted out Lowbeam.

'Then when I have spoken with Doctor Fortescue I will interview you next Mr Lowbeam.' Ravenscroft left the room, closely followed by Crabb, Roberts and Doctor Fortescue.

* * *

Once in the study, Ravenscroft and Crabb seated themselves behind the large desk, as Fortescue lowered himself into the leather armchair facing them, and Roberts took up his station near the door.

'Is all this really quite necessary, Ravenscroft? It is obvious that Sir John took his own life,' began Fortescue.

'I am not quite so sure, Doctor,' replied Ravenscroft, as Crabb opened his pocketbook and began writing.

'Well it is obvious to me — single bullet through the temple, door locked; I just don't see how it could have been otherwise.'

'There was no suicide note.'

'Not all those who commit suicide leave notes behind them,' protested Fortescue.

'You said yourself that Sir John was neither depressed nor in pain. '

'Patients sometimes have a way of concealing those symptoms. And how do you explain the locked door? I presume the window was locked and bolted?'

'It was, but there is the possibility that whoever killed Sir John may have locked the door behind himself upon leaving, and then dropped the key inside the room this morning,' suggested Ravenscroft.

'That hypothesis would be extremely difficult to prove.'

'Could you tell us exactly what happened this morning, after Travers the footman was sent upstairs to see what had happened to Sir John?' asked Ravenscroft, ignoring the last remark.

'Well, we were all in the dining room at the breakfast table.'

'You say all of you. Could you be more specific? Was everyone present?'

'Yes, I believe so. Oh no, not quite everyone. Mr Nightingale was still in his bedroom, I believe.'

'So Mr Nightingale was not present at the breakfast table?'

'That is so.'

'But everyone else was present when March came to tell you all the bad news.'

'Yes.'

'Please continue, Doctor Fortescue. What happened next?'

'I immediately sprang to my feet and followed March upstairs to the study.'

'Did anyone follow you?'

'Yes. Mr Critchwood, Mr Lowbeam and Monsieur Hubert followed quickly on behind me. We thought it better if the women remained downstairs.'

'Lady Critchwood and Miss Nightingale stayed in the dining room?'

'That is so. Lady Critchwood was obviously greatly shocked by the news. Miss Nightingale stayed with her to lend support and comfort.'

'So you, Mr Critchwood, Mr Lowbeam and Monsieur Hubert all followed March up the stairs and into the study.'

'That is correct.'

'What happened next?'

'I made a quick examination of the body, in case Sir John was still alive. March said that he had instructed Travers to send the coachman to the police station in Bromsgrove, so I thought it better if the others went away from the room and waited downstairs.'

'Do you recall if any of the others said anything, or acted in a strange way?' asked Ravenscroft.

'I don't understand.'

'Did anyone go through Sir John's papers, for instance?'

'No. I remember that shortly after we entered the room, Mr Critchwood nearly fainted. It was evidently quite a shock for him to see his father dead like that. We supported him for a while and then I instructed Lowbeam and Hubert to take him downstairs, and to see that he had a stiff drink.'

'You remained with the body until our arrival?'

'Yes. March stayed in the room with me for a while, then he excused himself saying that he would wait downstairs for the police to arrive.'

'While you were waiting did anyone else come into the room?' continued Ravenscroft.

'Yes. Mr Nightingale did.'

'When did he enter the room?'

'Some fifteen minutes or so after the others had left.'

'What did he say, or do?'

'He said that he had heard the terrible news when he had gone down to the breakfast table, and had been sent to make further enquiries by Lady Critchwood. I assured him that everything was in hand, then he went away to join the others.'

'Did he come right into the room?'

'Yes. I remember that he was hesitant at first to enter the room, which is quite understandable. Some people find death rather unsettling. Then he recovered his nerve and came closer. We talked briefly about how terrible this was, especially as the tragedy had taken place so close to Christmas, and how it would be difficult for Lady Critchwood to come to terms with her husband's death, but that Miss Nightingale was doing all she could to comfort her. That was all.'

'Well, Doctor Fortescue, your evidence has been most helpful to us,' said Ravenscroft, leaning back in his chair.

'Then I take it that I may go?'

'Certainly. Where may we contact you again, should we need to do so?'

'My practice is in New Road, approximately halfway up the hill on the left-hand side. My wife and I live above the surgery,' replied Fortescue, rising to his feet. 'I must say, Inspector, that all this is rather taking things too far. I still believe that poor Sir John took his own life, and I shall enter that fact on the death certificate.'

'Of course, Doctor, that is your prerogative.'

Roberts opened the door as Fortescue made his way out of the room.

'Interesting,' said Ravenscroft. 'The good doctor was adamant in his belief that his patient had killed himself, while providing no evidence to suggest that Sir John was suffering from any medical or spiritual complaint.'

'You think he could have killed Sir John?' asked Crabb.

'He certainly had plenty of opportunity to cover his tracks and plant that key on the floor, but I cannot see why he would have wanted Sir John dead. He has known the family for years, so what possible motive could he have had to kill Sir John now?'

'His account rather rules out both Lady Critchwood and Mary Nightingale.'

'Yes, neither of them came into the room, so they did not have the opportunity of returning the key, but Mr Critchwood, Mr Lowbeam and this Monsieur Hubert are all possible suspects. Then there is still March and Travers — and of course we must not forget Mr Nightingale. Just what were he and his sister doing here? Sir John implied that he hardly knew Nightingale, but if that was the case, why invite him and his sister to dinner, and ask them to stay the night? I find it strange that Nightingale was not at the breakfast table when March came down with the news. Was he waiting for an opportunity to slip into the room, before Fortescue and the others made their way up the stairs — or did he drop the key on the floor, unnoticed by Fortescue, when he entered the room later?'

'His sister could have killed Sir John, and then passed the key on to her brother to dispose of later,' suggested Crabb. 'They could both be in this together.'

'I suppose that is another possibility. We need to know more about Sir John's personal affairs. Roberts, ask Mr Lowbeam to join us now, if you please.'

'Yes sir,' replied the constable.

* * *

'I hope this won't take long, Ravenscroft,' said the solicitor as he strode into the room. 'I have an urgent appointment with an important client in my offices in thirty minutes.'

'Please take a seat, Mr Lowbeam. I can assure you that we will be as quick as we can,' said Ravenscroft. 'We are given to understand that you are a solicitor in Bromsgrove.'

'That is so. Lowbeam, Sanders and Forrester have practised in the town for well over two hundred years. I personally am the fourth generation of my family to be a partner in the firm.'

'And you are also the family solicitor for the Critchwood family?'

'That is correct.'

'For how long have you been the family solicitor?'

'I personally have represented Sir John for over thirty years, but the family's association with the practice goes back a number of generations, I believe.'

'So you would know everything about Sir John's personal and financial affairs?'

‘I would not exactly say that. Sir John was a very secretive man, in some respects. He liked to keep different aspects of his life in separate compartments, if you understand what I mean.’

‘I do. I presume that Sir John left a will?’

‘Yes. He liked to revise his will every three or four years. The last revision was made earlier this year.’

‘And who are the chief beneficiaries of his estate?’

‘I am afraid I am not at liberty to tell you that at present. It would not be in order to disclose any of the will’s contents until it has been read to the family, after the funeral has taken place. There is such a thing as client confidentiality and a strict protocol to follow,’ said Lowbeam firmly.

‘Oh, come now, Mr Lowbeam. Sir John is dead, and this is a murder enquiry,’ protested Ravenscroft.

‘I was given to understand that the poor man had committed suicide.’

‘We are keeping all lines of investigation open. It may be that someone had a grudge against Sir John?’ suggested Ravenscroft.

‘I was not aware of that, although I suppose you are likely to upset one or two people if you are involved in the business world.’

‘Like Mr Troth?’

‘Ah well, I do believe there had been some difficulties there,’ admitted Lowbeam.

‘Go on.’

‘Sir John had recently formed a new company. He wanted to buy a large parcel of land outside the town, at Charford, to build a number of houses.’

‘Nearly a hundred, we are given to understand,’ interjected Ravenscroft.

‘Well, yes, I suppose so,’ answered Lowbeam somewhat surprised by Ravenscroft’s line of questioning.

‘Are you a member of this new company?’

‘Good heavens, no. I try to keep away from anything like that. To tell you the truth, Sir John did ask if I wanted to be a member of his new company, but I declined. He was having some difficulty in persuading others to join, but then again I think he was probably also hoping to undertake the business on his own account.'

'He would then have been able to keep all the profits for himself. But I understand that Troth was unwilling to sell his share of the Charford lands?'

'So I believe.'

'And without that land, the project could not go ahead?'

'I suppose so.'

'Do you think that Sir John was upset by this turn of events?'

'It must have affected him.'

'So much that he became depressed and took his own life?'

'I could not say. I knew he was annoyed about the lack of progress of his scheme, but whether it was enough to cause him to kill himself, I would not know. As I have said, Sir John was a very private man.'

'Can you tell us anything else about Sir John's financial affairs?'

'He did not always confide in me. I was Sir John's solicitor, not his accountant.'

Ravenscroft smiled. 'But you must have gained some impression of the state of Sir John's financial affairs. We gather that Old Dodford Manor is heavily mortgaged, and that Sir John owes a great deal of money.'

'I am afraid I cannot enlighten you any further on that point, Inspector. All I can tell you is that things were not as well as they might have been.'

'What can you tell me about the Bromsgrove Gas Light and Coke Company?' asked Ravenscroft realising that the solicitor was unlikely to divulge anything more concerning Sir John's land purchase activities.

'Only that Sir John was its managing director. It was started about twenty years ago. It was very much Sir John's main project.'

'Were you on the board of the company?'

'No, certainly not. As a solicitor it is important that I remain impartial in the business affairs of the town.'

'Let us return to Sir John's will. It may be vitally important to the solving of this case if we were to know who stood to benefit from Sir John's death,' Ravenscroft persisted.

Lowbeam paused for a moment as he stared at Ravenscroft, then issued a heavy sigh before speaking. 'Very well. Most of the estate and title goes to his son, Christopher, with provisions made for Lady Critchwood during her lifetime. March and Travers have been left two hundred pounds each.'

'That is very generous,' remarked Crabb, looking up from his notebook.

'Both men have been loyal family retainers.'

'I wonder if you could tell me what happened after Sir John had retired for the evening? It was about ten o'clock, I believe?'

'Yes, we had all been talking and smoking in the drawing room. Sir John went upstairs at around ten. Lady Critchwood had already retired for the evening. Miss Nightingale sat reading for a few minutes before she too went upstairs. Doctor Fortescue, Monsieur Hubert, Mr Critchwood and Mr Nightingale played cards for a while, while I read a book.'

'And how long was that for?'

'About forty or fifty minutes, I would say. Then Fortescue broke up the foursome, saying he was tired. Mr Critchwood and Mr Nightingale went up a few minutes later. Hubert and I helped ourselves to another brandy and cigars before we too retired.'

'What time would that be?' asked Crabb.

'At about eleven thirty, I think. I went up alone, leaving Hubert still smoking in the drawing room.'

'What happened when Mr March told you that Sir John was dead this morning?'

'We all rushed upstairs after March and Fortescue. We thought it best if the ladies remained downstairs.'

'You say all of you rushed upstairs, except for the ladies?'

'Yes, that is just what I have said.' Lowbeam was starting to sound annoyed at the detective's continual questioning.

'That would be Monsieur Hubert, Mr Critchwood, and Mr Nightingale?'

'Yes, or rather no. Mr Nightingale had not yet come down to breakfast.' The solicitor consulted his pocket watch. 'Is that all? I really must insist that I leave now.'

'Yes, thank you, Mr Lowbeam, you have been of valuable assistance to us. Where is your practice, should we need to interview you further?'

'It is at the top end of the High Street, a half-timbered property with an overhang.'

'Does the name Conningsby mean anything to you? Eustace Conningsby?'

'No, I don't think so, but why do you ask?'

'That was the name of the man who was found dead on the railway line yesterday morning.'

'Yes, I remember reading about it. Such a terrible business.'

'He wasn't giving much away,' said Crabb when the solicitor had left the room.

'Why is it that solicitors always speak in the same way, never wishing to commit to an opinion, lest it be used against them at a later date?'

'Perhaps you should have gone in for that line of work, sir?' teased Crabb.

'I believe it pays quite well, and you are not out in all weathers. I am sure he could tell us a lot more about Sir John's affairs, if only he was so inclined.'

'He confirmed what Fortescue told us about the events of earlier this morning.'

'Yes, and if what he is telling us is the truth about last night, we now have an idea of what happened in this house. Lady Critchwood went up first, Sir John himself retired at ten, closely followed by Mary Nightingale. Doctor Fortescue, Mr Critchwood and Mr Nightingale all went upstairs before eleven o'clock.'

'Time for any one of them to have killed Sir John in his study,' suggested Crabb.

'Then Lowbeam himself went up at around eleven thirty,' added Ravenscroft.

'That could have been too late by then. Sir John would already have been up there for an hour and a half. Had Lowbeam wanted to kill Sir John, he would have been leaving it rather late.'

'And last of all there was this Monsieur Hubert; he must have gone up even later. I must say he interests me.'

'Shall we have him in next?' asked Crabb.

'No, I think we will talk with March. He has been Sir John's land agent for a number of years. Perhaps he can enlighten us further about his master's activities. Roberts, will you ask Mr March to come and see us? Then I would like you to go downstairs and interview the rest of the servants. Record their names, find out how long they have worked here, what they were doing last night, and also whether they saw anything unusual yesterday evening.'

'Yes, sir.'

* * *

'Sit down, Mr March, if you will,' instructed Ravenscroft. 'This is a terrible business. Can you think of any reason why Sir John would have taken his own life?'

'None that I can think of.'

'Had he been unwell or seriously concerned about matters lately?'

'No,' replied the agent bluntly.

'So his death has come as a surprise?'

'Of course it has,' snapped March.

'I take it you were not present at last night's dinner party?'

'That is so.'

'May I ask you to describe your movements yesterday evening?'

'Why? Am I under suspicion?' retorted March.

'We have to account for everyone's movements last night,' said Ravenscroft, seeking to placate the agent.

'Once the guests had arrived, at around seven, I left Sir John and went back to the lodge, where I live, after first eating with the servants in the servants' hall. I remained there for the rest of the night.'

'You live alone?'

'Yes.'

'So there is no one who can confirm your account?'

'Of course not,' retorted March. 'Look, what is all this?'

'And can you tell us your movements this morning?' asked Ravenscroft, raising his hand to prevent any interruption.

'I got up at around six thirty, came over to the house, had breakfast with the servants, then went into my office, until Travers came down with the news that the master had not slept in his bed, and that the door to his study was locked. We then went upstairs, and I forced the door open. The rest you know.'

'How long have you been Sir John's land agent?'

'For nearly twenty-five years.'

'And what does that involve?'

'I manage the estate for Sir John. I combine this with the duties of gamekeeper. I sometimes drive the master around in his carriage, and carry out various other duties, as and when required.'

'Did you visit Mr Troth recently?'

'I am sorry, I don't quite see what this has to do with Sir John's death.'

Ravenscroft observed that his last question had visibly shaken the land agent.

'We visited Mr Troth, and he told us that last week he received a visit from yourself and some of Sir John's men. A fight apparently broke out. Would you like to tell us what you were doing there, Mr March?'

'Sir John wanted to purchase some land in Charford.'

'To build a great number of houses,' interrupted Crabb.

'Yes. Mr Troth's land lies in the centre of the proposed development. Sir John had offered the man a good price for the land, but Troth refused. Sir John merely asked me to go there to make an improved offer and to see if the man would see reason,' said March, recovering his composure. 'Unfortunately Mr Troth was not in a mood to listen. An altercation took place. He attacked one of my men. I went to his aid. Troth was unfortunately hit in the face. We apologised and left. That is all. There was nothing to it.'

'I see. Did you know that Sir John was in financial difficulties?'

'No. Sir John never confided in me regarding anything of a financial nature.'

'Are you sure about that?' asked Ravenscroft.

'I have just told you that I know nothing about Sir John's financial affairs,' replied March firmly.

'That will be all for now. I wonder if you would be so kind to ask Travers to step up here.'

March stood up and gave Ravenscroft a stern glance before leaving the room.

'He certainly had the opportunity to kill his master yesterday evening, after Sir John had gone upstairs to his study, and before all the others had retired for the night,' said Crabb.

'Indeed, but why? I cannot see why he would have turned against his employer after all these years. Even if he knew that Sir John intended to leave him two hundred pounds in his will, I cannot think that he would murder for that sum of money. Furthermore, why would he have killed old Mr Stebbins and Eustace Conningsby? No, it just does not add up.'

'Do you believe him when he said he knew nothing about Sir John's financial affairs?'

'Not for one minute. As Sir John's land agent he must have been privy to the estate's financial accounts. I wonder why he did not admit that fact.'

Ravenscroft's deliberations were interrupted by a knock on the door.

'Come in,' shouted Ravenscroft.

'You asked to see me, Inspector,' said Travers.

'Yes Travers, do take a seat.'

'I would rather stand, if you don't mind,' replied the footman.

'As you wish. How long have you been in Sir John's employ?'

'I have been with the family for nearly five decades now. I came here as a stable lad in Sir Marcus's time.'

'Sir Marcus was Sir John's father?'

'Yes. He died about forty years ago.'

'I see.'

'I then became a footman, a role which I have continued since then. I also combine my duties with that of butler.'

'Did your master ever confide in you regarding either his state of health or concerning his financial affairs?' asked Ravenscroft, realising that the old retainer might be able to provide him with the additional information he was seeking.

'No. Sir John was a very private man. He was in remarkable good health. There was a riding accident some five years ago, but Sir John had made a good recovery.'

'So you would say that he was not unduly worried or anxious at the time of his death.'

'No, he was his usual self.'

'Did you know that Sir John's financial standing was not as it should have been?'

'As I said, Inspector, Sir John never confided in me,' replied Travers, looking away.

'What was the talk amongst the servants?'

'There was some idle gossip that Sir John was finding things difficult, but I did not pay too much attention to it.'

'Let us turn to the events of yesterday evening. Tell us what took place in this house,' said Ravenscroft.

'Sir John's guests arrived at around seven. I showed them into the drawing room and served them drinks. Dinner was served at eight precisely. Sir John was a very punctual man. I waited at table, after which the ladies retired to the drawing room, while the gentlemen smoked and talked for a while. Later they joined the ladies. Lady Critchwood went upstairs shortly afterwards, and Sir John followed at around ten.'

'Did Sir John always retire to his study at that time?'

'Yes. As I have said, Sir John kept to a regular routine. He liked to work on his research papers for an hour or two before going to bed.'

'Did you see Sir John again after he went into his study?'

'No.'

'Was Sir John in the habit of locking the study door, when he retired at night?'

'No.'

'Was there any reason why he should have done so yesterday evening?'

'No. I can only think that he did not wish to be disturbed, while he . . .' Travers' voice trailed away as he looked sadly down at the floor.

'Sir John's study and bedroom are in the old part of the house, are they not?' asked Ravenscroft, quickly changing the subject.

'Yes, Inspector. That part of the house was built in the sixteenth century, I believe. It formed part of the original Old Dodford Manor. The rest of the house was built in the last century.'

'Please continue with your narrative.'

'Shortly after Sir John had retired to his study, Miss Nightingale went up to her bedroom. The men continued talking and playing cards until a quarter to eleven, when Mr Fortescue left the company. Mr Critchwood and Mr Nightingale went up a few minutes later, and shortly afterwards Miss Nightingale's bell rang.'

'What did she want?' asked Crabb, looking up from his writing with interest.

'There was no one else to see to her. When I went up to her room, she complained of being cold, and asked if I could bring up some more wood and coal. I said that I would. I went down to the cellars, and brought them back to her room.'

'How long did all this take?' asked Ravenscroft, looking at Crabb.

'About five minutes.'

'What was Miss Nightingale doing when you entered her room?'

'She was sitting on a chair reading a book.'

'So she was not dressed for bed?'

'That is correct.'

'Did you notice anything unusual in the room?'

'No, although now that you ask, I did think her request was rather strange.'

'Strange? How was that?'

'Well the room was quite warm. There was quite a blaze in the hearth. We usually make sure that there is enough wood and coal in the bedrooms, but she must have used up all the supply, and no doubt wanted to ensure that the room would not get too cold during the night.'

'I expect that was it,' smiled Ravenscroft. 'Where is Miss Nightingale's bedroom in relation to the old wing where Sir John's study is?'

'At the end of the corridor, where the old original building ends.'

'Please continue with your narrative. What happened after this incident?'

'I went downstairs to the living room, where Mr Lowbeam and the French gentleman were still talking and drinking. Mr Lowbeam went up a few minutes later.'

'What time was that?' asked Crabb.

'At eleven thirty. I remember the clock chiming in the hallway. I asked Monsieur Hubert if there was anything else he required. He said no, so I retired to my quarters.'

'Leaving the French gentleman to finish his drink and cigarettes?'

'That is correct.'

'When was the front door locked last night?'

'It must have been around a quarter to nine. I locked it myself, while the family and their guests were finishing their dessert.'

'And obviously no one else had entered the house before that time, other than the guests?'

'That is correct.'

'What about the other doors?' asked Crabb.

'There is only one other entrance, through the kitchens, and I locked that myself at around nine o'clock. If anyone had entered that way before then, cook would have seen them. I cannot believe that the master would have killed himself. If someone did kill him, I hope that you will find whoever was responsible,' said Travers.

'We will do our best, Mr Travers. You can be assured of that.'

The retainer gave a little bow before he left the room.

'He confirms what the others have told us already,' said Crabb.

'Yes, but that was interesting about Mary Nightingale asking for more fuel for her fire, despite the room being warm. I wonder if that was a diversion to ensure that the footman was out of the way, giving enough time for either her brother or herself to enter Sir John's study and kill him.'

'That must be a strong possibility,' agreed Crabb.

'But it would be the deuce to prove.'

'Shall we have the Nightingales in next?'

'No. Let us see what this Monsieur Hubert has to say for himself. I wonder what this foreign gentleman is doing in Sir John's house.'

* * *

The Frenchman seated himself in the comfortable armchair, brushed an invisible hair away from the knee of his immaculate trousers, and reached into his coat pocket to retrieve a silver cigarette case.

'Monsieur Hubert, I would be grateful if you could outline for us your movements yesterday evening,' asked Ravenscroft.

'Pardon? I do not understand — outline my movements?' replied the Frenchman with a puzzled expression on his face, as he took out a cigarette and tapped it on the side of the case, before lighting it.

'If you could tell us what took place last night.'

'Ah yes. I arrived for dinner at around seven o'clock, then I ate the dinner, and afterwards we smoked and talked,' smiled Hubert. 'Oh yes, and we played cards.'

'What time did you retire?'

'It was just after twelve, I think.'

'You were the last to go upstairs?'

'Yes. Monsieur Lowbeam, he went just before me.'

'Did you go straight to your room?'

'Yes,' replied Hubert before exhaling, and then running his fingers along his waxed black moustache.

'And this morning?' asked Ravenscroft, watching the smoke from the Frenchman's cigarette slowly drifting up towards the ceiling.

'I came down to breakfast at eight o'clock, and, *bon Dieu*, all this terrible thing! Poor Sir John had killed himself.'

'Have you known Sir John for very long, Monsieur Hubert?'

'*Non*, only for two or three weeks.'

'How did you meet?'

'I met Sir John at his London club.'

'What sort of things did you talk about?' asked Ravenscroft, realising that the Frenchman was not going to be particularly forthcoming in his answers.

'What do the English talk about — the weather, the horses, the cricket; it is always the weather.'

'But that is not why Sir John invited you here for dinner last night?'

'Ah, I can see that you are not so easily fooled, Inspector. Sir John and I had a common interest — gas!'

'Could you elaborate further?'

'I am the managing director of the Loudéac and Brittany Gas Lighting Company. Sir John is the managing director of the Bromsgrove Gas Light and Coke Company.'

'Where is Loudéac?' asked Crabb looking up from his notebook.

'It is in the centre of Brittany. It is a very famous town. We supply all the gas to the towns like Rennes, Dinard, Saint-Malo, Quimper and many more.'

'So Sir John invited you here simply because you had a common interest in gas?' asked Ravenscroft, as the Frenchman took another long draw on his cigarette.

'Ah, I can see how you are a dog without his bone, as they say. You have caught me red-handled! Sir John and I were on the point of a grand business deal for our two concerns.'

'Go on, Monsieur,' encouraged Ravenscroft.

'My company is seeking to expand its interests. We have money to invest. We would like to supply the gas and the electricity to several of your English towns,' replied Hubert, flicking the ash from his cigarette into an ashtray with one hand, while again gently brushing his knee with the other.

'So you were seeking help from Sir John in this business venture?'

'Ah, you have it, Inspector! We need more than help. We seek a business partner who is English.'

'I see, and you wanted Sir John to invest some capital in this new business enterprise?'

'Yes of course. Any investment made by Sir John would be more than met by my own company, and would yield good results in the years ahead.'

'And that is why Sir John invited you here — so that you could discuss this business venture?'

'That is correct.'

'Bur now unfortunately Sir John is dead.'

'It is a problem. It is such a terrible thing to have happened. It is very sad.'

'So what will you do now, Monsieur Hubert?'

'I must return to Brittany, but first I will speak with the new Sir Christopher. He may be interested in investing, who knows?'

'He knows of your business plan?'

'Oh yes, he was present at the preliminary meeting with Sir John.'

'I have to tell you Monsieur Hubert, that if Sir John had still been alive I do not think that he would have been able to have invested in your new business company.'

'*Pardon?* I do not understand,' asked Hubert, looking somewhat alarmed.

'Sir John is heavily in debt. I cannot see how he, or his son, could have funded your business plan. Perhaps he was under the impression that your company would be able to provide the funds for the venture? That is why he may have invited you here.'

The Frenchman grew agitated. 'This is terrible! I have been deceived! *Non*, this is not possible. Sir John, he said that he had plenty of money.'

'I am sorry, Monsieur Hubert, to be the bringer of such bad news.'

'*C'est terrible!*' sighed the Frenchman.

'So I am afraid you will have to find another English backer,' said Ravenscroft.

The Frenchman gave another loud sigh and extinguished his cigarette. 'That I must do, but first I must return quickly to Brittany.'

'I would be grateful if you would not go just yet, until we have concluded our investigation into Sir John's death.'

'I have been invited to stay a day or two, until after Christmas.'

'Do you believe any of that, Crabb?' asked Ravenscroft, once Hubert had left the room.

'It does seem rather too convenient.'

'My thoughts exactly, but it seems unlikely he could have murdered Sir John. Remember, he was in full sight of other people in the drawing room last night for the first hour and a half after Sir John had left the company to go to his study, and did not go up to his room until nearly twelve, by which time Sir John was already dead, according to Fortescue's estimate. Much as I find the man of dubious character, I cannot see him as our murderer. I think it is time we called up Mr Nightingale and his sister.'

* * *

Peter Nightingale escorted his sister to the chair facing Ravenscroft, and then accepted the other chair, which Crabb placed alongside.

'Thank you, Mr Nightingale, Miss Nightingale,' said Ravenscroft.

'This is a very sad business. I would not have thought that Sir John would have done such a thing,' said Peter Nightingale.

'So you think that Sir John committed suicide?'

'It looks that way, unless you know anything different.'

'May I ask why Sir John invited you here?' asked Ravenscroft, avoiding the last comment.

'Sir John and I have undertaken some business transactions in the past, mainly to do with insurance,' replied Nightingale, looking at Ravenscroft warily.

'Oh come now, Mr Nightingale, I think you have more of a connection than that. When I visited here two days ago, Sir John was conducting a meeting in this very room. You were one of those present. Are you a member of the board of the Bromsgrove Gas Light and Coke Company, Mr Nightingale?'

'Er, yes, I do have shares in the company.'

'Were you also involved in Sir John's project to build a large number of houses on land at Charford?' asked Ravenscroft, noting the other's unease.

'I know nothing about that. Look what is the point of all this? Are we under suspicion?'

'Everyone who was in this house last night is under suspicion, Mr Nightingale, until I am satisfied that I have satisfactorily concluded my investigation into Sir John's death. We understand that you were in the habit of borrowing money from Mr Stebbins the bookseller. I have here that gentleman's account book and your name appears more than once. The last entry is for fifty pounds. Quite a substantial sum, I think you would agree?'

'I know nothing about that.'

'Oh come Mr Nightingale, it is down here in black and white. It is no use pretending otherwise. I mean to get at the truth. Did you, or did you not, borrow money from Mr Stebbins?' said Ravenscroft, raising his voice.

'Well, what if I did?' cried out an annoyed Nightingale. 'I borrowed the money to purchase some shares in Sir John's new company to build those houses at Charford. It is not against the law. There is no harm in that, surely?'

'There is no harm at all Mr Nightingale, although it would have helped us if you had told us this earlier.'

'I didn't think it was your concern.'

'Would you like to tell us what happened last night?' asked Ravenscroft.

'What do you mean?'

'If you could both run through your movements, I would be obliged.'

'We arrived here for dinner just before seven,' Mary Nightingale's voice was quiet.

'You had also been invited to spend the night here?'

'Not initially. But you have seen how bad the roads are out here, and what with the unpleasant weather, Sir John and his wife extended their invitation to stay the night.'

'Can you tell us what happened after dinner?'

'My sister and Lady Critchwood withdrew to the drawing room, while we men sat smoking and talking in the dining room. We later joined the ladies. Some of us played cards for a while,' said Peter Nightingale.

'At what time did Sir John retire?'

'I think it was just after ten. I believe you went up soon after, did you not, my dear?' asked Peter Nightingale.

'Yes,' confirmed Mary, looking wistfully down at the floor.

'And you, Mr Nightingale?'

'I carried on playing cards, before going upstairs. I think it must have been sometime before eleven o'clock. I slept soundly, I must say.'

'Did anything happen after you retired for the night, Miss Nightingale?'

'No. I read for a while and then I went to bed.'

'You did not call for Travers, the footman, to fetch more fuel for your fire?'

'No, I don't think so. Oh yes, of course. I remember now. I had been reading and the room was getting quite cold. I had used up all the wood and coal, so I asked Travers to replenish the scuttle.'

'Travers says the room was quite warm.'

'Then he must have been mistaken. I am also a very light sleeper. I often wake two or three times during the night, and sometimes find it difficult to go to sleep again. I wanted to be sure that the room would be kept warm,' answered Mary Nightingale in a quiet, formal manner. 'These old houses can be quite cold and draughty.'

'When I visited you yesterday you told me that you had never heard of Eustace Conningsby, and yet you seemed quite distressed when I informed you that was the name of the dead man found on the railway line.'

'I was naturally upset by your sudden news, but I can assure you that I have never heard of this gentleman.'

'Miss Nightingale, why are you lying to us?' said Ravenscroft, raising his voice.

'Look here, Ravenscroft—'

'I think you knew Eustace Conningsby, Miss Nightingale,' went on Ravenscroft, ignoring Peter Nightingale's interjection. 'Why don't you tell us the truth?'

'I take exception to all of this!' shouted Peter Nightingale rising to his feet and glaring at the detective. 'My sister has answered your question. She does not know this Conningsby. Why can't you accept the word of a lady?'

'Miss Nightingale, the truth, if you will,' demanded Ravenscroft.

'It is alright, Peter. We must tell the inspector everything.' Mary reached out to touch her brother's arm. 'He will only find out the truth later if we don't tell him now.'

'If you must,' said Peter Nightingale, giving out a loud sigh of resignation, as he slumped back into his chair.

'Eustace Conningsby and I were once engaged to be married.'

'I see. Please go on.'

'It was over fifteen years ago. We were living in Islington, in London, then. I met Eustace at a ball. He was considerate and amusing. After one or two other meetings he proposed to me, I accepted and we were engaged,' said Mary.

'But you did not marry?' asked Ravenscroft noticing the sadness in her eyes.

'No. I was only seventeen. My parents did not consider it a suitable match.'

'Oh, tell them the truth Mary, for goodness' sake. Conningsby was a penniless wastrel. When our father found out he was furious and forbade him to see Mary ever again,' said Peter Nightingale. 'It was as simple as that.'

'So you see, Inspector, I did once know him, and yes I may even have loved him, but it was not to be.'

'Did you ever see Mr Conningsby again after the engagement was ended?'

'No. He always said that one day he would be rich, and that he would then come back for me, but he never did.'

'Did he ever write to you?'

'No, there was nothing. So you see how upset I was when you told me that he had been found dead on the railway line,' answered Mary Nightingale, tears beginning to form in her eyes. 'It brought it all back to me. I have such painful memories. I am so sorry, Inspector.'

'Did Conningsby know that you were now living in Bromsgrove?'

'No.'

'So he had not written to you, telling you that he was coming to the town?'

'No, how could he? He did not know that we had moved here.'

'I see, well thank you Miss Nightingale. You may both go now,' said Ravenscroft.

Nightingale rose from his chair with an angry look at the detective. 'All this was quite unnecessary, Ravenscr—'

'Oh, just one more question, Miss Nightingale,' began the detective.

'Really, Ravenscroft, can't you see how all this has upset my sister?' protested Peter Nightingale.

'When we called upon you yesterday, when you opened the door, I think you were expecting to see Mr Critchwood,' said Ravenscroft.

'I don't know,' said a distressed Mary Nightingale avoiding Ravenscroft's eyes.

'And after we left, as we were walking away, we observed Mr Critchwood entering your house.'

'Mr Critchwood comes to me for piano lessons,' said Mary, recovering her composure. 'He is a pupil of mine.'

'Is that all, Ravenscroft?' demanded Peter Nightingale.

'Yes, thank you both. That will be all for now, but we may need to talk with you again,' said Ravenscroft.

'Insufferable,' muttered Peter Nightingale, placing his arm round his sister's shoulder as the pair left the room.

'I don't know why people make our job so difficult, Tom. If only they told us the truth in the first place, instead of resorting to evasion and denial, it would all be so simple.'

'At least we now know why Mr Nightingale was borrowing money from old Mr Stebbins,' said Crabb.

'Yes, but again why did we have to force the truth out of him? Just what is he hiding? How heavily involved was he in Sir John's financial dealings?'

'He had the opportunity to enter Sir John's study unobserved, while his sister was distracting Travers with her request for more fuel for her fire.'

'In which case, Tom, they were both in league in their plan to kill Sir John, but if that is the case why would they have done so? I can see no reason for them to have committed the crime, but then of course there is the question of Eustace Conningsby. I am not so sure that Mary Nightingale did not know that her former lover was coming to Bromsgrove. I wonder if that was the reason why she never married, because she secretly hoped that one day Conningsby would return.'

'Perhaps he had become wealthy in the intervening years?' suggested Crabb.

'Or was he coming to Bromsgrove with the intention of gaining wealth?'

Ravenscroft and Crabb's deliberations were rudely interrupted by a loud tap on the door.

'Come in,' shouted Ravenscroft.

Constable Roberts entered the room. 'I've done what you asked, Inspector.'

'Good man. What can you tell us?'

'Well, Sir John does not exactly employ a large number of servants, although the cook says there were more until a year or so ago.'

'Interesting,' added Ravenscroft.

'They believe that Sir John has fallen on hard times, and that is why he had to let some of them go. There is a cook, over seventy, I would say, who has been with the family for over forty years, a scullery maid of eighteen, and a stable lad. That is all.'

'I see what you mean, Roberts.'

'They all live in. There are also two or three men who work on the land, under March's supervision, but they all reside in the village.'

'Did any of the servants notice anything unusual yesterday evening?' asked Ravenscroft.

'No, sir. No one was seen entering the house, other than Sir John's guests earlier in the evening. The say that March left the house after taking supper with them, and that Travers locked both the front and back doors during the dinner.'

'Thank you, Constable. So what do we have now, Tom? Which of these people killed Sir John, and why?'

'You would have to rule out the Frenchman, as he did not go up to bed until nearly twelve o'clock,' suggested Crabb.

'I am inclined to agree with you, although there is something not quite right in Monsieur Hubert's story. He interests me, but I do not know why. I think we can rule out both Travers and March. Although they had plenty of opportunities to kill their master, and we only have their word for it about how they broke into the room this morning, I cannot see why they would want to kill Sir John. They only stood to gain by a few hundred pounds, and both appear to have been loyal retainers. What do you make of Lowbeam?'

'He seemed very reluctant to answer our questions in a direct manner,' answered Crabb.

'And Doctor Fortescue, what do you think of him?'

'He seemed more than ready to accept that Sir John had taken his own life.'

'Yes. But why would either Lowbeam or Fortescue want to kill Sir John? Both are respected men in the town, neither of whom was involved in Sir John's business affairs, so again I cannot see how they would benefit from his death. Which brings us back to the Nightingales, and their connection with the Critchwood family, with Eustace Conningsby, and with old Mr Stebbins. But again, I cannot see why they would have killed any of these men. Damn!' Ravenscroft brought his hand down hard on to the desk before him. 'Confound it! We have spent nearly all morning questioning these people and we are now no further forward. They all seem likely suspects, and yet appear to be completely innocent of the crime. We are missing something here, and I cannot see the wood for the trees. It is all very frustrating.'

'There is always young Mr Critchwood,' suggested Crabb.

'Yes, we have not questioned him yet, but what motive did he have to kill his father? All he stood to gain was the title, a heavily mortgaged property, and a failing business empire. No, I do not see him as our killer. What on earth is that noise outside?'

Suddenly the door to the room was rudely flung open.

'Inspector Bullman!' Ravenscroft rose quickly from his seat.

'What the devil is going on here, Ravenscroft?' asked the red-faced policeman, striding into the room, with a uniformed constable following swiftly on his heels.

'Sir John Critchwood is dead,' answered Ravenscroft.

'I know that. Constable Masters here tells me that someone came to the station this morning with the news. Why wasn't I informed?' growled the inspector.

'With all due respect Bullman, we were told you were attending the court in Worcester,' protested Ravenscroft.

'Case finished yesterday.'

'Both roads and rail were blocked last night — you have surely only just arrived back in Bromsgrove? Anyway, you asked me to take over the case when we found that dead man on the railway tracks.'

'What's that got to do with Sir John?'

'We found the bookseller's account book. He loaned a quite substantial sum of money to Sir John.'

'Yes, yes, but what has all that to do with you being here?' asked an irritated Bullman.

'It is rather a long story,' sighed Ravenscroft.

'Well you better get on with the telling of it.'

During the next few minutes, Ravenscroft recounted how their investigations had identified the dead man as Eustace Conningsby, and how Mr Stebbins's account book had led them to Old Dodford Manor, before describing how he and Crabb had arrived there earlier in the day to view the body and to question the suspects.

'Well, have you found out who killed Sir John or not?' asked Bullman, when Ravenscroft had finished his account.

'We have one or two suspects,' answered Ravenscroft, trying to sound optimistic.

'It seems to me, Ravenscroft, that you have nothing. You don't even know if Sir John was murdered. You say that Doctor Fortescue believes it was suicide?'

'That is his opinion, but what man intending to kill himself fails to leave a suicide note and locks himself in his room?'

'It seems perfectly possible to me,' muttered Bullman.

'Furthermore he was shot in the left temple, and Sir John was right-handed.'

'Is that all you can come up with?' laughed Bullman. 'You really believe that suicides think in a rational way? Then there is the locked room to consider.'

'The killer could have dropped the key on the floor when no one was looking,' voiced Crabb.

'But you can't prove that, nor can you prove that this Conningsby fellow was also murdered. He could have hit his head on the rails falling from the last train of the day.'

'I believe he was murdered,' emphasised Ravenscroft.

'But you can't prove that, man. You are clutching at straws; same as all that speculation over the missing papers. Have you seen those papers?'

'No, of course not,' protested Ravenscroft.

'Exactly, that proves my point.'

'But I do believe that was why Conningsby came to Bromsgrove. Once we have the missing papers we will know who killed Mr Stebbins, Eustace Conningsby and Sir John.'

'I tell you, Ravenscroft, we have already arrested Mr Stebbins's killer. He was caught red-handed at the scene of the crime. I have no doubt that he will hang next week after being found guilty by a good jury.'

'I don't think he did it,' protested Ravenscroft.

'Where's your evidence, man? It is just as I thought. Ravenscroft,' said Bullman, adopting a quieter, almost patronising tone, 'it's Christmas Eve. You look tired. Why don't you go home? It has stopped snowing and the trains are running again. Get out while you can. I'll sort things out here. Leave it to me.'

Ravenscroft looked at Bullman. 'Very well. We will come back after Christmas Day.'

'Constable Roberts here will take you to the station. I'm sure you'll see things clearer after a good rest.'

* * *

'How long has it been now, Tom?' asked Ravenscroft, as the two men faced one another in the railway carriage.

'Five years, sir, since we first met on a train like this,' answered Crabb.

'We have been through a lot together since then, and solved quite a few crimes, but I must say that this must be one of the most difficult cases we have ever encountered. Three men cruelly struck down, and we are no further forward in apprehending the perpetrator. Perhaps Bullman was right all along.'

'You don't really believe that.'

'I don't know what to believe any more. Perhaps it is time I retired,' Ravenscroft sighed.

'You have a few more years yet, sir, and anyway, you would not know what to do with your time,' said Crabb encouragingly.

'We will see. Enough of all this, let us put the case on one side for at least one day. Christmas is nearly upon us, and I can see that we are approaching your station. Give my best wishes to that good sensible wife of yours, and those glorious children. Have a good Christmas, Tom, and we will meet up again at nine on Boxing Day,' said Ravenscroft, as the train drew into Malvern Wells Station.

'And Christmas greeting to you, and to Mrs Ravenscroft and the children,' said Crabb, smiling.

The two men shook hands warmly, before Crabb stepped on to the platform.

As the train gathered speed and the tunnel came nearer, Ravenscroft leaned back in his seat, gave a deep sigh, and, realising how tired he was, closed his eyes and tried to dismiss the events of the last few days from his mind.

* * *

'A Happy Christmas to you, sir,' said a cheery-faced old gentleman, a few minutes later, as Ravenscroft alighted from the train at Ledbury Station.

Ravenscroft returned the greeting, and, turning up his collar against the cold, trod on the snow-covered pavement as he made his way down towards the Homend. It was already dark but the dim gas lamps of the town lighted the way ahead, offering the promise of a better world.

Reaching the edge of the town, he pushed open the door of a tiny toyshop.

'Good evening, Inspector,' said the shopkeeper as Ravenscroft stepped into the warm interior.

'I trust you have the items for me,' said Ravenscroft.

'Of course.' The shopkeeper dipped down beneath the counter. 'Here we are. I've wrapped them as instructed.'

'Excellent.'

'I am sure your children will love them,' beamed the shopkeeper.

'I know they will be delighted with them.'

'May I wish both you and your family the compliments of the season?'

'Thank you — and a happy Christmas to you,' returned Ravenscroft, picking up the two parcels from the counter.

As he made his way down the main street of the town, Ravenscroft quickened his pace as he observed that several of the shopkeepers had already begun to close their premises.

Finally he reached the shop he was looking for, and peered anxiously into the window. Yes, the item he was seeking was still there, and he was relieved to see that the shop had not yet closed.

'Good evening, Inspector Ravenscroft,' said the lady behind the counter. 'Are you looking for a last-minute gift from our winter jewellery range?'

'The necklace in the centre of the window, with the red stones,' smiled Ravenscroft.

'A wise choice, if I may say so,' said the shopkeeper, reaching into the window, removing the item and placing it on the counter.

'That will be just fine. I have been admiring it for a week or more. I am sure that Mrs Ravenscroft will like it a great deal.'

'Shall I wrap it for you, sir?'

'That would be most kind.'

A few minutes later, Ravenscroft crossed over the Market Place, where the last goose was being sold by a solitary stallholder to an eager schoolboy, and turned into Church Lane. His boots sounded on the icy uneven cobbles as he made his way up the narrow lane, passing by the occasional lights flickering in the various windows.

And then he reached the cottage he was looking for, but instead of going up the path, he paused for a moment, and looked towards the brightly lit window. There was his wife fixing a star to the top of the tree, smiling as the two children ran around excitedly.

Then for a moment he saw again an earlier Christmas with his parents, where there had always been an empty chair at the table, and when nothing was ever said, but those gone had never been forgotten. Then he remembered the many Christmas days he had spent alone in those cold rooms in London, when time had seemed to stand still, and he had longed for the industry of the next day to take away his loneliness.

Suddenly Lucy caught sight of him and waved, the door was thrown open with excitement, and there was warmth and light, and joy — and as Ravenscroft made his way up the path he gave thanks that he was the luckiest man alive.

CHAPTER EIGHT

LEDBURY, CHRISTMAS DAY

'Samuel! Samuel!' called out a familiar voice.

Ravenscroft woke with a start. 'Oh, I'm so sorry, my dear, I dozed off. How long have I been asleep?'

'For nearly an hour,' replied Lucy returning to her seat by the fire.

Ravenscroft stretched. 'Surely not that long? I only closed my eyes a few minutes ago.'

Lucy looked at the old grandfather clock in the corner of the room. 'Fifty-five minutes, to be exact.'

'I'm sorry, it must have been the effects of that goose, or the second helping of that excellent plum pudding — and then the warm fire and your gentle reassuring presence. Any man would succumb to such pleasures. How are the children?'

'Susan took them up thirty minutes ago. They were quite tired after all the excitement.'

'I will look in on them shortly.'

'So it was a white Christmas after all,' said Lucy.

'Yes, unfortunately that meant I had to spend a night in that awful inn, but thank goodness Tom and I were able to leave Bromsgrove and be home in time for Christmas. I have to admit, there was a time when it looked as though we would be snowbound in the town for the remainder of the festive season.'

'Richard was so pleased with that jigsaw you gave him, and little Arthur simply adored all those Noah's Ark animals.'

'I am pleased,' smiled Ravenscroft, moving upright from his previous slumped posture, and readjusting his spectacles.

'And thank you so much for the necklace. It is quite beautiful and I shall treasure it for ever.'

'And I must thank you for these fine crimson slippers. I must say that I have never worn such comfortable footwear. I believe I shall never leave the house ever again.'

'But you must; you have to catch the murderer of the old bookseller, and save young Stebbins.' Lucy picked up her needlework.

'Yes. I feel rather guilty sitting here tonight with my loved ones around me, while poor Stebbins is still languishing in that cold damp cell in Worcester with the threat of a death sentence hanging over him.'

'You must not reproach yourself, Samuel. I am sure that you have done everything that you can at present.'

'Yes, but that is not enough. Since I went to Bromsgrove two men have been murdered in a brutal fashion, and we are no further forward in discovering the truth about this matter.'

'Well, those Nightingales are certainly not to be trusted, from what you have told me,' emphasised Lucy.

'They were certainly not very cooperative, but I cannot see a reason why they would have committed all these murders.'

'If only someone had noticed who had dropped that key in the study.'

'Yes, that would have solved everything.'

'You are sure that is what happened? Could there have been another way in which Sir John could have been murdered?'

'The great locked room mystery! Well, the windows were certainly locked and bolted from the inside, and I doubt if anyone could have climbed up that narrow chimney, and anyway there was the remains of a fire in the hearth.'

'So what will you do next?' asked Lucy.

'Go back to Bromsgrove tomorrow and take up the case again, unless of course Detective Inspector Bullman has not already arrested someone for the crimes during my absence.'

'He does not sound particularly helpful.'

'I suppose I can understand his attitude. I probably wouldn't take it too kindly if some inspector from another area came here to Ledbury and elbowed in on one of my cases. I must ask him why his name is in old Mr Stebbins's account book.'

'You don't think he could have killed all those people?' joked Lucy.

'Probably not, but policemen have been known to stray from the straight and narrow. Anyway, enough of all this, let us see what is happening in the local paper.'

'There is an article on page five which might interest you.'

Ravenscroft opened the paper. 'Ah, here we are — "Carol Singers Slip on the Ice."'

'No, it is not that story.'

'"New Year's Eve Party in Ledbury Postponed?"'

'Now you are being silly,' reprimanded Lucy.

'"Bogus Clergyman Arrested in Hereford."'

'I thought it would amuse you.'

Ravenscroft read aloud from the newspaper.

> 'The notorious criminal Arthur Collingwood has been arrested after he tried to sell a number of items of church plate at a local jeweller's shop in Hereford. We understand from our Hereford correspondent that Collingwood had been impersonating a Church of England clergyman for over a year. He had apparently been in the habit of visiting a

number of churches in the area, calling himself the Reverend Septimus Severn, where he ingratiated himself with the local clergymen, gaining their trust, and familiarising himself with the church artefacts, before returning at a later date to steal the said items. Further investigations have shown that Collingwood has a long history of impersonating men of the cloth, and has spent at least two terms of imprisonment in Wakefield and Manchester prisons. Collingwood will stand trial next week in Hereford. A heavy sentence is to be expected.'

'It is a wonder he got away with it for so long,' said Lucy.

'Talk about condemning a man before he is tried. "A heavy sentence is to be expected." What happened to being innocent before proven guilty?'

'Have you ever encountered him?'

'What, either Arthur Collingwood or Septimus Severn? I can't say that I have had that pleasure, although I do recall going to Bosbury last March where two silver plates had been stolen from the vestry.'

'You did not catch the culprit?'

'Obviously not, but it at least proves the point that the police cannot solve everything, although in a great many cases it is only a matter of time before the habitual criminal overreaches himself and is apprehended.'

'Well I think I rather secretly admire poor Arthur Collingwood. At least he showed some initiative and enterprise.'

'I can't believe you said that, Lucy. Would you have me let all the criminals I have arrested go free because they displayed a talent for crime?' Ravenscroft joked.

'I suppose you don't know who to trust these days. People are sometimes never who they say they are. Why only the other day a strange-looking man came calling at our house,' began Lucy.

'What was that you said?' Ravenscroft leant forward eagerly.

'That last week a strange-looking man had called at our house.'

'No, not that, you said that people are sometimes never who they say they are. Of course — Albert Spanswick!' exclaimed Ravenscroft, jumping up out of his chair.

'Who is Albert Spanswick?' asked Lucy, somewhat taken aback by her husband's sudden excited behaviour.

'Albert Spanswick is one of the greatest villains who ever lived upon this earth. Why did I not see it before?'

'See what before?'

'That Albert Spanswick is alive and well, and currently in Bromsgrove.'

'What are you going to do?'

'I shall travel over to Bromsgrove tomorrow — and arrest Albert Spanswick!'

CHAPTER NINE

BROMSGROVE, 26 DECEMBER

'I cannot believe that I did not recognise Albert Spanswick when we interviewed him,' said Ravenscroft as he and Crabb sat in the train the following morning.

'Have you ever encountered him before?' asked Crabb.

'Not in person.'

'Then how do you know it was Spanswick?'

'His reputation was well known at Scotland Yard. Fraud, deception, misappropriation of funds — you name it, Spanswick's hands were all over it. He was on the most wanted criminal list. At the yard we had a photographic gallery of all the most prominent criminals.'

'Begging your pardon, sir, but it has been a long time since you were at the Yard.'

'I know. That was why I failed to recognise him. It was only last night that my memory was stirred, and I suddenly realised that we had interviewed Spanswick at Old Dodford Manor.'

'It is good for us that you did remember.'

'In my days at the Yard, Spanswick operated in London and the Home Counties, but it looks as though he has now widened his interests to the Midlands. Spanswick's speciality was in trying to sell shares in new London theatres, promising that those who contributed would have a special seat dedicated to them, which they would be able to use whenever they wanted, and that they would have a share of any profits the shows made. Of course, he had no connection to the theatres. Then he sold fake shares in rare orchids in the hot house at Kew Gardens, with the promise that lucky subscribers would have a special plant named after them. In fact, there was no end to his schemes, but always when he was in the Yard's grasp he would suddenly disappear for a year or more, before reappearing under a different name, in a new disguise, and with a new scheme with which to dupe foolish investors.'

'He sounds quite a colourful character.'

'We must arrest him in time before he flies the nest. I sent an urgent telegram to Bullman at the police station this morning, before breakfast, asking him to meet this train upon its arrival at Bromsgrove Station. My only hope is that Bullman has received the telegram before this train reaches Bromsgrove.'

'Why didn't you tell him to arrest Spanswick as soon as possible?'

'I want to be there in person when we confront Spanswick. I want to see what he has to say for himself when we charge him.'

'Do you think he could be behind all these murders?'

'He could be. I would put nothing past him. I am sure he is involved in all this. Fortune may be on our side at last,' said Ravenscroft enthusiastically.

* * *

A few minutes later, the train pulled into Bromsgrove Station and Ravenscroft opened the carriage door and stepped briskly on to the platform.

'Good morning,' said Constable Roberts, coming forward to meet the two detectives.

'Good morning Roberts. You got my telegram obviously,' said Ravenscroft. 'Where is Detective Inspector Bullman?'

'I think it might be his day off, sir. I was in two minds whether to send a message for him to come here, but then I thought it would be better to meet you first.'

'You did right, Roberts. I think we can let Inspector Bullman enjoy his day of rest.' Ravenscroft was relieved. 'Now, Roberts have you seen any of the suspects we interviewed at Old Dodford Manor before Christmas?'

'No, sir.'

'Then I hope we may be in time, unless Spanswick has left on the early-morning train, although he had no reason to suspect that anyone had recognised him. None of our suspects are here, I think.'

'No.' Roberts looked around. 'There are one or two farmhands waiting over there with the milk churns, and an old woman sitting on the bench.'

'Good, nobody connected to the case, then. When is our train due to leave the platform to go on to Birmingham?'

'I believe it will be another five minutes, sir.'

'Then let us wait behind that milk cart and see if our man makes a last-minute appearance to get on to the train.'

'Yes, sir, but who are we waiting for?' asked Roberts.

'Only for one of the greatest criminal minds of this century,' said Ravenscroft as the three men secreted themselves behind the milk churns.

'You really think he will try to leave now?' asked Crabb after two or three minutes had elapsed.

'If I was Spanswick, then that is just what I would do. The longer I waited to leave Bromsgrove, the greater the risk would be that someone would discover my true identity.'

'Look!' said Crabb, just as the stationmaster raised his whistle to his lips. 'Over there, a man has just walked through the entrance on to the platform, carrying a suitcase.'

'It is our quarry! Quickly, we must prevent him from getting on that train,' instructed Ravenscroft.

The man walked quickly towards one of the carriages — but as he reached for the door, Ravenscroft and his colleagues closed in upon him.

'Monsieur Hubert, you are leaving us too soon,' said Ravenscroft, placing his hand firmly on the carriage door to prevent it opening.

The startled Frenchman turned to face the detective. 'Inspector Ravenscroft?'

'I thought you were staying at Old Dodford Manor for a few days.'

'Indeed, but I have received an urgent telegram this morning that has called me back to London,' smiled Hubert. 'Now if you will excuse me, the train is due to depart.'

'Then it will leave without you, sir,' said Ravenscroft firmly.

'But this is not right,' protested the Frenchman as the stationmaster blew his whistle and raised his flag.

'Put the handcuffs on him, Crabb,' instructed Ravenscroft.

'Please, what is this? I do not comprehend.'

'You are coming with us to the police station, Monsieur Hubert. Or rather, I should say, Mr Spanswick.' Ravenscroft had a note of triumph in his voice.

'Pardon? I do not understand.' Hubert shook his head. 'Who is this Spatwick?'

'Spanswick,' emphasised Ravenscroft, as Crabb fastened the cuffs round the prisoner's wrists. 'My colleagues at the Yard have been after you for years, but before I send you off to them, I want to question you about three murders here in Bromsgrove. Put him in the cart, Roberts.'

* * *

Fifteen minutes later, Ravenscroft and Crabb faced their prisoner across a desk in one of the back rooms of Bromsgrove Police Station, as Roberts stood to attention by the door.

'Now then Spanswick you have a great many questions to answer,' began Ravenscroft.

'I do not understand all of this. My name is Pierre Hubert. I am a citizen of France. I have never heard of this Spangwick, Spatwick person. It is obvious that you have made a mistake. You are confusing me with someone else.'

'Very good Spanswick, but it just won't do. It won't do at all. Why don't you admit that you are Spanswick, and save us all a great deal of time.' Ravenscroft removed his spectacles and cleaned them on his handkerchief.

'No. I keep telling you that my name is Pierre Hubert,' protested the Frenchman.

'Do you have any papers on your person that can prove that?'

'*Non*. My papers are at home.'

'Ah yes, in Loudéac.'

'That is so.'

'Loudéac, the headquarters of your Brittany Gas Lighting Company,' said Ravenscroft in a mocking tone.

'*Oui*, that is correct.'

'Well it might interest you to know that I have looked up this Loudéac, and it is a small, insignificant town in the middle of nowhere.'

'*Non*, Loudéac is in the centre of Brittany. It is very important that we can cover the whole of Brittany from there, rather than from the coast,' protested Hubert.

'What nonsense. I think you met Sir John Critchwood in London, and that you then told him a long story about how your bogus company was looking to acquire a financial partner, with a view to expanding your empire here in England,' suggested Ravenscroft, leaning forwards and directly confronting his prisoner. 'Is that not so? In truth, there is no Brittany Gas Lighting Company. You only wanted to cheat Sir John out of a great deal of money, just as you cheated all those theatregoers in London into buying non-existent seats in London theatres, and all those unsuspecting investors into having rare flowers named after them in Kew Gardens.'

'*Non. Non.* This is all wrong. My name is Pierre Hubert. I am a French businessman visiting your country. You are mistaken. This is terrible.'

'Is that why you killed Sir John Critchwood? Because he uncovered your crooked plan, and was threatening to turn you over to the police authorities?' continued Ravenscroft, ignoring his prisoner's denials.

'No, why would I kill Sir John? I thought he shot himself?'

'No, Spanswick, Sir John was murdered, and his killer locked the door behind him, and then dropped the key on the study floor the next morning when nobody was looking.'

'I do not understand all this. How could I have killed Sir John, when I was downstairs in the living room until after twelve o'clock?'

'Yes, it would seem that you had a good alibi, but of course you and Sir John had agreed to meet in private in his study, after everyone else had retired for the night.'

'This is, how you say, preposterous!' exclaimed Hubert. 'You have no proof for all this nonsense. These old houses are full of hiding places. Anyone could have hidden themselves away and killed Sir John.'

'Why did you kill Eustace Conningsby? Was he on your trail? Did he follow you to Bromsgrove with the express purpose of confronting you, and that is why you killed him as well, so that your shoddy little plan could still go ahead?' said Ravenscroft, raising his voice, and feeling that if he continued with his questioning the impostor would shortly admit his guilt.

'Who is this Conningsby? I have never heard of him.' Hubert was becoming agitated.

'What I can't quite make out at the present time is why you also killed Mr Stebbins.'

'Who is this Mr Stebbins?' laughed the prisoner. '*Bon Dieu!* Who are these people?'

'So you deny killing Sir John Critchwood, Eustace Conningsby and Mr Stebbins?'

'Of course. This is all so ridiculous! It is obvious that you have mistaken me for someone else. Look, Inspector, there are several business associates of mine both in London and in Brittany who can prove my identity. If you would grant me leave to go, I promise to return within seven days with these people, who will confirm my account that I am Pierre Hubert.' The Frenchman began to rise to his feet.

'Roberts,' instructed Ravenscroft.

'You are staying right here, sir.' The constable stepped forwards and pushed the prisoner firmly back into his seat.

'I protest most strongly at your behaviour. I shall go to the French Embassy in London and they will make a formal complaint to Scotland Yard,' said Hubert angrily.

'But you are not going anywhere, Spanswick, other than the confines of a very small cell, until I have secured evidence to convict you of all these terrible crimes.'

'This is all wrong. You will regret this. I tell you I am Pierre Hubert,' said the prisoner, raising his voice in desperation.

'We will see. Before we entered this room today, you may have seen that I was writing something on a piece of paper, which I then gave to one of my constables. He has just visited the telegram station, where he has paid to send a telegram to a colleague of mine at Scotland Yard. Shall I tell you what that telegram said?'

The prisoner shrugged his shoulders before sinking back into his chair.

'I told them that I had you, Spanswick, and that they were to send me details of your criminal record, together with a recent photograph they have on file. I am sure the Yard will be very pleased to know that I have you in custody. Until that time arrives, you will remain in a cell. Then we shall see who is telling the truth,' said Ravenscroft.

'No, no, this is not right,' shouted Hubert.

'Take him down, Constable,' instructed Ravenscroft.

'I tell you I am not Albert Spanswick!' blurted out the prisoner.

'Who said Spanswick's Christian name was Albert?' declared Ravenscroft, bringing his fist down on the table.

'You did!' stuttered the Frenchman.

'No. I only said "Spanswick." I never said "Albert Spanswick,"' replied Ravenscroft, staring at his opponent with a look of satisfaction on his face.

'Damn you, Ravenscroft.' The prisoner covered his face with his hands.

'It's all over, Spanswick. Tell us the truth.'

The prisoner said nothing. Ravenscroft looked up at the clock on the wall.

'Come on, Spanswick, we haven't all day,' urged Ravenscroft after ten seconds had elapsed.

'Alright, I admit it. Well done, Inspector!' Spanswick clapped in a mocking manner.

'So tell us the real reason why you were at Old Dodford Manor,' asked Ravenscroft, pressing home his advantage. 'And please drop that terrible French accent.'

'Very clever, Inspector, you have caught me fair and square,' said Spanswick speaking in a cockney accent, and giving a feeble nervous laugh. 'I'll tell you everything I know. Do you mind if I have a cigarette first?'

Ravenscroft nodded and Spanswick reached into his pocket and took out the silver cigarette case he had used at Old Dodford Manor.

Crabb passed over a box of matches.

Spanswick lit the cigarette, inhaled deeply and leaned back in his chair. 'I admit that I came to Old Dodford Manor with the intention of persuading Sir John into investing in my company.'

'Which is entirely bogus,' interrupted Ravenscroft.

'Oh come on, Inspector, less of the high moral tone. Everyone has to make a living.'

'How did you first meet Sir John?'

'It was at his London club. I know the doorman there. He's an old acquaintance of mine. He got me in. All I needed was to find someone who would be likely to invest in my scheme. That was when I saw old Sir John. I got talking to him. I could see that he was interested. I noticed the greed in his eyes. He was easy prey. We met again two days later. He had his son with him then, but I could tell that he had no more common sense than his father. They invited me down here for Christmas, saying we could conclude the deal. It was all set, but then it went wrong.'

'How do you mean it went wrong?'

'Silly man went and killed himself, didn't he? What a thing to do. Still, I thought, maybe not all was lost. That son of his looked anxious to do the deal. Then you turned up and started asking all those probing questions, saying that the old man had no money after all. So then I thought, I'd get out of here as soon as I can, but then another inspector turns up asking questions all over again, and by the time he'd let us leave the blessed weather turned bad and snowed us in for Christmas. I could not leave until this morning, and that was when you apprehended me at the station.'

'It all sounds very straightforward, except that I do not believe a word of it,' said Ravenscroft.

'I've told you the truth. I own up to the fact that I am Albert Spanswick, but I don't do murders. It is not my kind of thing. Why would I want to kill the old man? What would I gain from it?'

'Why did you kill Eustace Conningsby and Mr Stebbins?' asked Crabb.

'I've never heard of those two people. Who are they? Look, I admit that one or two of my business concerns in the past may not have worked out as I would have wished, but I don't go round killing people, Inspector Ravenscroft. You has to believe that,' pleaded Spanswick, flicking ash away from his cigarette.

'You have a criminal record that stretches from here to London and back, and for all I know you may well have killed one or two people, or more, along the way.'

Spanswick adopted a more defensive tone of voice. 'If you don't believe me, there's nothing I can do about it, but if you think I murdered all these people, where is your proof?'

'We don't need any proof yet. All we need to do is to put you in a cell, until your details arrive from the Yard, then we will see what information they can add to our enquiries. Of course you could save us both a great deal of time and trouble, and just tell us the truth,' said Ravenscroft.

'I have told you the truth, Inspector, but you choose not to believe it. For the last time, I never murdered anyone,' answered Spanswick, staring directly at the detective.

'There's no more to be said. Take him down to the cells, Roberts.'

'You are making a big mistake, Ravenscroft,' said Spanswick as Roberts placed the handcuffs around his wrists. 'This is all wrong.'

'Well at least we have managed to apprehend a notorious criminal,' sighed Ravenscroft, once the prisoner had left the room.

'You think he was telling us the truth?' asked Crabb.

'He may not have murdered our three victims, but there is no way of telling at the present time. He certainly gave a creditable performance as Pierre Hubert and I have no doubt that he was intending to swindle Sir John out of a great deal of money, although it would not have done him much good as the landowner had no funds to invest. Once he realised this, did he then kill Sir John out of anger, disappointed that all his efforts had come to nothing? I can't really see that. Spanswick is a fraudster and a swindler; I do not quite accept that he is a killer as well, but then Spanswick is a very clever man, and that he may be fooling us. All we can do at present is leave him in the cells, and wait for that file and photograph to turn up from the Yard. They may be able to provide us with the missing information we need to complete this jigsaw.'

'I am inclined to agree with you. I don't think Spanswick is our man.'

'Then who is, Tom? One of the people in the house that night must have shot Sir John — but which one? Or have we been looking at this from the wrong perspective? We know what everyone was doing for the two hours after Sir John retired to his study, but . . .' His voice trailed away.

'Yes, sir?' asked Crabb, puzzled.

'It was something that Spanswick said just now. He said that "these old houses are full of hiding places; anyone could have hidden themselves away." I think we should go back to Old Dodford Manor.' Ravenscroft jumped up eagerly from his seat. 'I want to have another look at that study.'

CHAPTER TEN

BOURNHEATH

Ravenscroft looked up at the dark sky and drew his scarf tighter around his neck. 'It is getting colder. This snow will soon freeze, I am sure.'

'We'd best not wait until nightfall before we depart, otherwise we will have to spend another night at the Black Cross,' said Crabb, urging the horse along the narrow lanes that led out of the town towards the village of Bournheath. Constable Roberts had remained on duty at the police station, but had made the police trap available to the visiting detectives.

'Heaven forbid. Another night in that cold draughty room with only the past inhabitants of the inn for company will be the end of me.'

'What are you expecting to find at Old Dodford Manor?'

'A hiding place that could have concealed the murderer. When we arrive, say nothing that may give anyone cause for suspicion, just say that we want to take another look at the room where Sir John was killed.'

A few minutes later, Crabb brought the police trap to a halt outside the main entrance of Old Dodford Manor.

Crabb handed the horse's reins to the stable boy. Christopher Critchwood met them at the door.

'Inspector, I am glad that you have come,' said the anxious young man. 'It is Monsieur Hubert. He seems to have left in somewhat of a hurry. He did not come down to breakfast, and when I made enquiries of the stable lad he said that he had been instructed to take him to the station earlier this morning.'

'I have to tell you, Mr Critchwood, that we have Monsieur Hubert in custody. We arrested him at the railway station this morning while he was attempting to join the Birmingham train,' said Ravenscroft.

'Arrested him? I don't understand.'

'Well, it seems that your French guest was not all that he seemed. He is in fact a well-known fraudster called Albert Spanswick.'

'Good Lord!'

'His intention in visiting you here was to try to persuade you and your late father to join a fraudulent business venture of his. I trust that you have not agreed to any such financial involvement?'

'No . . . Well, he did try at first, but once my father died in such a dreadful way he seemed to lose all interest. He was quite determined to leave. All day yesterday he hardly said anything to us, and had the weather been better I am sure he would have left then rather than have waited until this morning. You say he is a well-known fraudster, Inspector?'

'I am afraid so.'

'Gosh, it seems as though we have had a lucky escape.'

'Indeed.'

'So, how are your investigations proceeding? '

'As well as can be expected,' replied Ravenscroft, trying to sound optimistic.

'You know, I don't really believe that the old man killed himself like that. It was not in his character. He was involved in so much, and he had a great deal to live for. I think that you would agree with me, Inspector.'

'I am not at liberty to say at present, Mr Critchwood.'

'Now you have told me that Hubert was really a villain, it must also be obvious that he is my father's killer.'

'We have him in the cells as we speak, and shortly one of my colleagues from Scotland Yard will be here, when we will question him further. In the meantime, I wonder if my colleague and I may take another look at your late father's study?' asked Ravenscroft.

'Yes, of course. Travers can take you up there.'

'Thank you, sir. Oh, just one more question. The other day after we had visited Miss Nightingale at her house in Bromsgrove, I believe I may have seen you also calling on the said lady?'

'Er, yes, that is correct,' replied Critchwood nervously.

'May I ask the reason for your visit?'

'I was just calling upon them to ask if she and her brother were still going to dine with us later that evening. Is that all?'

'Yes, if we may see the room?'

'Travers, show these men up to my father's study if you would,' instructed Critchwood.

Ravenscroft and Crabb followed on behind the footman up the staircase and along the corridor that led into the older part of the building, coming to a halt outside the study at the end of the passageway.

Travers unlocked the door.

'I trust no one has entered this room since I was last here?' asked Ravenscroft as he and Crabb entered the study.

'That is correct, Inspector. I thought it best that the room should remain locked.'

'Thank you, Travers, you may leave us now. I will ensure we lock the door when we have finished.'

The footman gave the key to Ravenscroft and closed the door behind him as he left the room.

'Well, Tom, what do you make of that?'

'You mean Mr Critchwood giving us that story about calling on Mary Nightingale?'

'Yes. One of them is lying, but which? Mary Nightingale said that Mr Critchwood had come for a piano lesson, whereas he said he had merely called to make sure they were coming to attend the dinner party.'

'Do you think they could perhaps be romantically linked in some way?' asked Crabb.

'I don't know. There must be a fifteen-year age gap, or more, between the two of them, but then there is a twenty-year age difference between Mrs Ravenscroft and myself, so their situation is far from unusual. But why lie about it? Why not just tell us the truth?'

'It could be that Mr Critchwood is telling us the truth, and that Mary Nightingale would like their relationship to be stronger than it actually is, hence the story about him being her pupil.'

'An interesting theory, Tom. Anyway, it may have little bearing on this case. Lock the door. We don't want to be disturbed. Now, we know that the window was securely locked from the inside and that no one could have climbed up this narrow chimney, so which other way could our murderer have left the room? This part of the house dates back to the sixteenth century. I wonder whether the Critchwoods could have been of the Catholic tendency. Old houses like this often had hiding places where Catholic priests could hide from the authorities,' said Ravenscroft, surveying the room.

'There is this large cupboard in the corner,' suggested Crabb.

Ravenscroft walked over to the piece of furniture, opened its large doors and tapped the sides and bottom. 'It seems very solid, whereas this room has a considerable amount of oak panelling on its walls. Let us tap the woodwork. If there is brick or stone behind the wood then there should be little sound, but if there is a hollow space then the sound will be quite different. You take that wall, Tom.'

The two detectives set to their task.

'Tom!' called out Ravenscroft suddenly.

'You think there could be something there?'

Ravenscroft tapped again on a part of the woodwork. 'Listen. Do you notice the difference between here and, say, over here?'

'Yes, but there is no handle or other sign that there might be a hollow space behind the panelling.'

'If you were a Catholic living in this house in the sixteenth century you would not want anyone else to know that there was a hiding place just here. Now how would one gain access? I will put my shoulder up against it and see if it gives,' said Ravenscroft.

'Good Lord!' exclaimed Crabb as part of the woodwork gave way under Ravenscroft's shoulder, opening up into what at first sight appeared to be a small closet.

'This is where our priest hid from the authorities.'

'It is not very big,' remarked Crabb.

'People were a lot smaller then. There is just room for a man to stand, and I suppose there could have been a stool of some kind so he could sit.'

'It must have been very uncomfortable and dark. It is a wonder anyone could breathe in here.'

'You are right. But our priest would possibly not be in here for very long, just an hour or so while the authorities were searching the house, then when they had left he would emerge from his prison and conduct Mass with the people of the house, before moving on to the next Catholic residence. It was a way of keeping their faith intact.'

'So you think whoever killed Sir John might have hidden in here after the murder?'

'If he did, it would have been decidedly unpleasant. Furthermore, it does not explain how our killer could have got into the building in the first place. It was certainly well disguised; one piece of panelling amongst many. It must have been like this for four hundred years or more.'

'I wonder if Sir John knew that it was here.'

'If he did, he must have kept that knowledge to himself. Neither March, nor Travers, nor anyone else in the house, has mentioned its whereabouts to us.'

'How would our killer have known it was here?' asked Crabb.

'I don't know. Maybe all this is getting us no further forward, unless . . .'

'Yes, sir?'

'Light one of the candles and bring it over. I want a closer look inside this priest hole,' said Ravenscroft.

Crabb returned with a lighted candlestick.

'Hold it just inside, while I inspect the woodwork. Yes, it is just as I thought. This part of the floor is quite loose. I think I can slide it to one side. Give me the light,' said Ravenscroft enthusiastically.

'It's a flight of steps!' exclaimed Crabb.

The two men looked at one another in amazement.

'They appear to be going downwards. We had better see where they lead.'

'They are very narrow; it looks a bit of a squeeze.'

'I'll go first with the candlestick. You light another candle and follow on behind,' said Ravenscroft, stepping into the enclosed space.

Step by step Ravenscroft cautiously made his way down the steep narrow wooden steps, holding the lighted candlestick in front of him to illuminate the way, as Crabb followed on in the same fashion.

'We must have reached the lower level of the house by now, but the steps continue downward,' said Ravenscroft. 'Mind your head, Tom, there is little room here.'

'We must be under the house now,' remarked Crabb, protecting the candle flame from any sudden movement that could lead to its being extinguished.

'I think you are correct. Ah, I can see the bottom of the steps now. Yes, here we are.'

'It looks like a tunnel of some kind going away from the house.'

Both men lifted their candles as high as they could and peered anxiously into the darkness in front of them.

'I have heard of these old tunnels that were constructed as a secret way out of the building. I wonder where it leads?' said Ravenscroft.

'What is that on the floor?' asked Crabb suddenly.

'I don't know, it looks like a coin of some sort.' Ravenscroft brought his candle nearer as he reached down.

'Perhaps there is some treasure buried down here.'

'I don't think so. This is a silver shilling with our present queen's head on it. An 1887 Jubilee Head, if I am not mistaken. This means that someone has been down here in the last five years, and that this coin accidentally dropped out of their coat pocket.'

'Perhaps it belonged to our murderer?'

'Very likely; I am even more determined now to see where this tunnel goes to.'

Ravenscroft walked slowly forwards, his head bent below the roof, the light before him pointing the way, as Crabb followed closely behind.

'This seems to go on for ever. We must be well clear of the house by now. I think I might just have an idea where this tunnel is going to,' remarked Ravenscroft.

'As long as we get out of here soon,' said Crabb. 'This place sends shivers down my spine.'

'Here is the end of the tunnel,' announced Ravenscroft, suddenly coming to a halt. 'But there are some old stone steps going upwards.'

A climb of a dozen or so steps brought the two men into a small enclosed space.

'There must be a way out. Yes, look. Whereas these three sides seem to be made of bricks, this one consists of wood. Hold the candle a minute, Tom, and I will see if this gives way.'

Ravenscroft put his shoulder to the woodwork and a small space was slowly revealed. 'It appears to open out into a room of some kind. I think someone has put a large bookcase, or another piece of furniture, up against the entrance. I don't think it will give any more.'

'Let me try and squeeze through the gap. If I can get out, I can perhaps remove the obstacle,' offered Crabb, passing over his candlestick to Ravenscroft, before gradually inserting himself into the narrow space.

'Be careful, Tom, we don't know what is on the other side.'

'I'm through now, sir,' whispered Crabb. 'You're right, someone has covered the entrance with a bookcase. I'll try to push it to one side so you can get through.'

Ravenscroft waited as Crabb struggled to make the gap wider.

'That will do. I think I can get through now.'

'It's a small room,' said Crabb as Ravenscroft joined him. 'Where are we, sir?'

'If I am not mistaken, this is the chapel in the grounds of Old Dodford Manor. We caught sight of it as we made our way up the driveway when we first visited here. This anteroom is obviously where they stored things. The tunnel could have been here for centuries, with no one knowing that it was even here. When our killer returned here, after he had killed Sir John, then he made sure that the entrance was hidden by covering it over with the bookcase.'

'If our killer did use this way to enter Sir John's study, then it means that he cannot be one of the people staying in the house.'

'It would appear that way, but we cannot be certain that the killer did use this way on the night of the murder. It might be that someone else, perhaps even Sir John himself, came this way sometime during the past five years, and that it was he who dropped that coin, in which case the killer could still be one of our suspects,' said Ravenscroft, thinking out loud.

'But if the killer did use the tunnel, if it was an outsider rather than a guest, then that would suggest Troth. We know he hated Sir John because he was trying to buy up his land,' suggested Crabb.

'That must now be a strong possibility, but first we need to explore further.'

'What about March? He said he was in his cottage at the time the murder was committed. Perhaps he knew all about the existence of this tunnel and used it to gain access to the study?'

'That is another possibility that cannot be ruled out. Now, let us see if I am correct about our location. I believe that if we open the door on the other side of the room, we should find ourselves in the main part of the chapel itself.'

Crabb eagerly opened the door. Just as Ravenscroft had suspected, they were in the chapel.

'Well, it certainly looks as though it has never been used for centuries, although there is still some kind of rudimentary altar near the window,' said Ravenscroft, surveying the interior.

'Quite a damp, musty smell,' commented Crabb.

'It is also extremely cold. I suppose the place does not get much air or sunlight and has clearly been abandoned for many centuries. Early Norman, by the design of that window and archway.'

'Come and look over here, sir,' called Crabb excitedly.

'A tomb of some kind . . . Bring the light nearer. It is just as I thought, one of the Critchwoods, possibly either Sir John's father or grandfather, I would say by the design.'

'There are more Critchwoods here,' said Crabb.

'It seems as though we have found the final resting place of the Critchwood family, and I have no doubt that Sir John Critchwood will shortly be joining his ancestors. Shall we take a look at those tombs over there?'

'They seem much older.'

'They might date back to Norman times. I wonder if the Critchwoods came over with William the Conqueror? Some of them might even have gone on Crusades later. Good heavens!' exclaimed Ravenscroft as he bent down to read the lettering at the base of one of the tombs. 'See here, Tom, look at that name.'

'Conningsby!'

'Indeed. The earlier tombs are on this side of the chapel. This one is also a Conningsby.'

'And this one,' said Crabb.

'Do you know what this means, Tom?' said Ravenscroft, startled.

'That the Conningsbys were here before the Critchwoods?'

'Yes. So we now know the connection between the Conningsby and Critchwood families. I wonder if this was why Eustace Conningsby was visiting Bromsgrove. I think that old Mr Stebbins had somehow uncovered the connection between the two families — in which case, was Eustace Conningsby returning to his ancestral home?'

CHAPTER ELEVEN

BROMSGROVE

'Was that why Eustace Conningsby was killed — to prevent him from claiming his inheritance?' asked Ravenscroft.

'I wonder if he was killed and placed on that railway line by Sir John?' murmured Crabb.

'If that was the case then we could be looking for two murderers. If Sir John killed Conningsby, then who killed Sir John? This case becomes more complicated the more we unravel.'

'We are not going back through that tunnel?'

'No,' laughed Ravenscroft. 'No need to put ourselves through that again. If the front door of this chapel opens, then we will walk back to the house. It will be interesting to see how other people react when they see us walking up the path to the main entrance of the building again.'

'Thank goodness for that.' Crabb sounded relieved. 'I never did like confined places. It comes from being born and bred on a country farm, I suppose.'

'I would like to know a lot more about the history of these two families, in particular why the estate passed from the Conningsbys to the Critchwoods. If we can answer that question the whole case may well fall into place.'

* * *

'But . . . but I don't understand,' said the footman, taken aback by the sudden reappearance of Crabb and Ravenscroft at the main entrance to Old Dodford Manor. 'I thought you were both in the study?'

'We were. If you would care to take us back there now, Mr Travers, all will be revealed,' said Ravenscroft.

Ravenscroft and Crabb followed the footman up the main flight of stairs and along the corridor, pausing only when they reached the study, where the detective produced the key and unlocked the door.

'If you would care to look over there, Mr Travers.' Ravenscroft pointed towards the open panel in the wall.

'Good heavens. What is this?' said the footman, moving closer to the opening.

'It is a priest hole, but you will see that there is also a flight of steps, which leads to a tunnel, which in turns comes up in an anteroom of the old chapel. I take it that you did not know of its existence?' asked Ravenscroft.

'No. Never. I have lived and worked here for nearly thirty years, Inspector, and never knew that this was here.'

'Sir John never mentioned it to you?'

'No.'

'I say, what is all this?'

Ravenscroft turned round to see that the new speaker was Christopher Critchwood.

'We have uncovered a secret tunnel that leads to the old chapel,' said Ravenscroft.

'Gosh! This is something,' said the young man quickly coming forward and peering into the hiding place. 'Father certainly kept this quiet.'

'Are you in the habit of visiting the old chapel, Mr Critchwood?' asked Ravenscroft.

'Only been there once or twice. It is a miserable old place that I avoid as much as possible. It is usually kept locked. It's where all the old Critchwoods are buried. I expect that my father will take his place there now. What a gloomy thought! I'm not going to be buried there if I can help it. They can take me out to sea and tip me over the side when my time comes. That will be a far better place to end up.'

Ravenscroft smiled, amused by the young man's remarks. 'Did your father ever talk about the old chapel?'

'No, I don't believe that he did.'

'We found some Conningsby tombs inside the chapel. They appear to be much earlier than the Critchwood monuments. Can you tell us anything you know about the Conningsby family?'

'I can't say that I have ever heard of them.'

'So your father never mentioned anyone by the name of Conningsby?'

'As I said, I have never heard of these Conningsbys.'

'Mr Travers?'

'No, Sir John never spoke to me about them,' replied the old retainer.

'That is a pity. I would like to know more about the Conningsby family. Do you know of anyone in the area who might be able to assist us in our enquiries?'

'There is Mr Sadd. He is what you might call a local historian. He recently wrote a number of articles in the local weekly newspaper about Old Bromsgrove,' said Travers.

'Where does Mr Sadd live?' asked Crabb, taking out his pocketbook.

'Mr Sadd resides in the village of Fairfield. It is not far from here. If you go back to the main Stourbridge road you will find that it is the next village, in a northerly direction. Mr Sadd lives in a large red-bricked house called The Laurels.'

'I wonder what Mother will say when I tell her all about this secret route,' said Critchwood enthusiastically, looking again into the priest hole. 'This is all perfectly marvellous. We shall have some fun when my friends come to stay.'

* * *

Within the hour, Ravenscroft and Crabb were standing outside a large red-bricked house situated at the entrance to the nearby village of Fairfield. Brushing aside the snow that partially covered an old cracked wooden sign, Ravenscroft revealed the words "The Laurels. Cornelius Sadd. Visitors Only By Appointment" as Crabb secured the horse to the gate.

'It does not look as though our Mr Sadd has been out for a few days. There are no footsteps in the snow up to the main door,' said Ravenscroft as the two men made their way up the path.

Crabb gave a long pull on the bell, and receiving no reply repeated the action some seconds later.

'I think I can hear someone inside,' said Ravenscroft as the sound of someone drawing back a heavy bolt could be heard.

'Yes,' said a voice through the small gap.

'I presume that I have the pleasure of addressing Mr Cornelius Sadd,' said Ravenscroft.

'Go away. I'm busy. You will have to make an appointment,' said the voice.

'We are the police,' announced Ravenscroft quickly, before the old man could close the door.

'I don't care who you are, I'm busy. Come back tomorrow.'

'We urgently require some historical information.'

'What historical information?' asked the voice opening the door a little wider to reveal an old wizened face wearing a pair of metal-framed spectacles, and a high forehead that was surmounted by thick long flowing white hair.

'We are detectives carrying out investigations into a number of murders in the area, and we have been told that you are the only man who can provide us with the information we need,' said Ravenscroft, trying to sound as serious as he could.

'Historical information, you say?'

'Yes, sir.'

'You should have said so earlier. Well I suppose you had better come in then,' said the old man, opening the door wider.

'Thank you, sir.'

Ravenscroft and Crabb stepped into a dingy hallway, where the walls were covered with faded photographs, and where a large number of items of footwear were piled along the sides of the floor.

'You had better follow me,' instructed the old man as he began to shuffle his way slowly out of the hall and along a passageway, until he reached a room at the rear of the building.

'This is my study.' Cornelius Sadd, led the way into a room where piles of books and manuscripts covered the floor. 'Take a seat.'

Ravenscroft looked down at a large black cat that stared upwards at him in a disapproving manner.

'Jaspar!' Sadd raised his voice and clapped his hands together. 'Be away with you!'

The cat reluctantly gave up his seat, and after brushing past Crabb, left the room with a loud growl of disapproval.

'Oh, don't mind him. He is rather a petulant fellow, used to having his own way.' Sadd lowered himself gently into his chair behind a desk that was cluttered with yet more papers. 'Well, how can I help you?'

'My name is Detective Inspector Ravenscroft and this is my colleague, Detective Sergeant Crabb,' said Ravenscroft as he accepted the seat. 'We are looking into the deaths of a number of local people. I wonder if you knew Mr Stebbins, the book dealer in Bromsgrove?'

'Indeed I did. I have known him for close on forty years, in a professional capacity of course. He supplied me with many books and manuscripts, mainly to do with the town and its environs. I was very sorry to hear of his demise, but I was given to understand that an arrest had been made.' Sadd peered at Ravenscroft over the top of his spectacles.

'That is true. Did you know that Sir John Critchwood had also been murdered?'

'No. When did this happen?'

'It was just before Christmas.'

'Dear me,' said Sadd, nodding his head. 'What a terrible thing to have happened.'

'We have been looking into the case. Have you ever had any dealings with Sir John?'

'No. I know of him of course. The Critchwoods are quite a prominent family in these parts.'

'Have you ever visited Old Dodford Manor?'

'No, I don't believe that I ever have, although I have read a great deal concerning the history of the property.'

'I believe part of the building goes back to the sixteenth century?'

'Indeed, and some of it may be older than that. The chapel certainly is.'

'I wonder if your research has revealed anything concerning the secret priest hole that lies hidden within the property?'

'Oh, that old chestnut. There has always been talk about hidden hiding places, but no one has ever found them. Apparently in the sixteenth century the family were Catholic.'

'So we believe. Could you elaborate?'

'If you were a Catholic in the time of Good Queen Bess you were compelled to adopt the religion of the newly established Church of England, and were forbidden to hold the Catholic mass in your home. The king of Spain, who was a staunch Catholic, encouraged a number of priests to come over to England. These priests would travel from one Catholic house to another, holding secret masses with their inhabitants, keeping the faith alive, as it were, before moving on to the next family. The authorities were always on the lookout for them, of course. The priests were often forced to take refuge in the priest holes,' said Sadd, warming to his subject.

'Well, today we found the priest hole,' announced Ravenscroft, pleased that the old man had confirmed what he already knew.

'Good heavens. So the rumours were true. Where was it?'

'We found it behind some old wooden panelling in the upstairs study.'

'Yes, of course, that would be a most likely situation. So it was true after all,' Sadd chuckled. 'Well I never.'

'Furthermore, we discovered that the priest hole revealed a number of steps that took us under the building, and along a tunnel, until we arrived at the old chapel in the grounds,' continued Ravenscroft.

'This is all most extraordinary — a secret way from the house to the chapel? How very ingenious. It was obviously constructed so that the priest could make his way out of the building, while it was being searched, and make good his escape.'

'Has anyone ever recorded the existence of such an escape route?'

'Not as far as I can recall.'

'When we were in the chapel we found a number of tombs of the Critchwood family, but also some earlier monuments to the Conningsby family. I wonder whether you could tell us anything about that family.'

'Conningsby? Certainly; they were the original owners of Old Dodford Manor.'

'We thought as much,' said Crabb.

'The Conningsbys were quite a prominent family in the locality in medieval and Tudor times. One or two of them even went on the Crusades, I believe. It was Sir Rufus Conningsby who built Dodford Manor in the early sixteenth, or late fifteenth century. It stood on the site of an earlier building I understand. They were local justices of the peace, members of the Bromsgrove Court Leet, that sort of thing.'

'If the Conningsby family were the original owners of Old Dodford Manor, why are the Critchwoods living there now?' asked Ravenscroft.

'Ah well now, that is a very interesting story.' Sadd leant back in his chair. 'It all goes back to the early eighteenth century. When Sir Edmund Conningsby died, he left no male heir. His son and his wife had both predeceased him. There was only a daughter, Maud. In his will he left everything to her. Shortly before Sir Edmund's demise, Maud Conningsby married a local man by the name of Alan Critchwood. That was how the Critchwoods came to be the new owners of Old Dodford Manor,' said the historian, pausing to produce a large handkerchief, into which he gave a loud sneeze. 'Forgive me, it is Jaspar. He is always leaving loose hairs lying around.'

'Can you tell us anything else about this Alan Critchwood?'

'The Critchwoods were quite a lowly family. What you might call small yeomen farmers in the social order. I cannot think that Sir Edmund would have entirely approved of the match,' answered Sadd before giving another loud sneeze into his handkerchief.

'I see.'

'Anyway, Alan Critchwood seems to have done the right thing. Shortly after Sir Edmund's death, Maud gave birth to the first of three sons. The Critchwood line was securely established, and the Conningsbys were no more.'

'You say that Edmund Conningsby had no sons to inherit. Do you know whether there were possibly any other Conningsbys who might have been eligible to inherit the estate?'

'Well I don't know about that. There is always some distant cousin or nephew in these cases, but because Sir Edmund had made his daughter Maud, his heir, that was an end to the matter. I don't quite know how her eldest son acquired the title 'Sir'. Some kind of purchase could have taken place.'

'I don't suppose you know when Sir Edmund Conningsby made his will?' asked Ravenscroft, intrigued.

'Not off hand.' Sadd sneezed again before rising from his chair. 'But I may be able to tell you, if you could give me a minute.' He shuffled over to a nearby bookcase. 'Now let me see. Ah yes, here we are. Worcestershire Wills from the Ecclesiastical Courts,' said the historian as he ran his fingers along a line of books. 'This should help.'

'I am obliged.'

Sadd dropped the heavy tome down on to his desk, releasing a cloud of dust which rose into steadily into the air. 'Now let me see. Yes, here we are. Sir Edmund made his will in 1723.'

'And when did he die?'

'Six years later, if my memory serves me well.'

'And you say that his daughter married this Alan Critchwood shortly before his death?'

'Yes, that is so. Ah, I see what you are thinking, Inspector. You are wondering whether Sir Edmund made another will after Maud married Alan Critchwood. Well I am sorry to disappoint you, but we only have the original will of six years earlier naming Maud as his sole beneficiary.'

'But Sir Edmund could have made another will later naming a distant member of the Conningsby family as his heir and beneficiary?'

'He could have.'

'And if this will were to suddenly reappear, then it would make the earlier will null and void?' suggested Ravenscroft.

'Yes, I suppose so, but it would become rather a prolonged legal issue, not dissimilar to Jarndyce and Jarndyce in Dickens's *Bleak House*. I fancy the lawyers would do rather well out of it.'

'I don't suppose Mr Stebbins ever mentioned to you that he might have found this missing will?'

'No, but I have not seen the bookseller for over a year. I don't get out much these days.' Sadd gave another loud sneeze into his handkerchief.

'Well, Mr Sadd, you have been most informative,' said Ravenscroft, rising from his seat. 'I thank you for your time and patience.'

'Glad to have been of assistance. I will show you out.'

Ravenscroft and Crabb followed the historian into the hall, where the cat gave a loud hiss as they passed by.

'Jaspar, do behave! That is no way to treat our guests. You must excuse his behaviour, Inspector. Unfortunately he does not come from a particularly good line, but then we owners are chosen by these creatures, rather than the other way round, don't you think? We seem to have little say in the matter.'

Ravenscroft smiled and as the two men walked back to the trap, they could again hear the sound of loud sneezing from behind the closed door.

* * *

'Well, Tom, there we have it. I am convinced now that Sir Edmund Conningsby made a later will, naming another member of his family as his heir apparent. Such a will would have removed Maud Conningsby and Alan Critchwood from the legacy. But somehow the will went missing, and Maud inherited. That must have been how the Critchwoods gained possession of the manor. I think that old Mr Stebbins came across this second will and was able to track down Eugene Conningsby's address in London. That was why he wrote to Conningsby telling him that if he came to Bromsgrove he would gain something to his advantage. However shortly after writing the letter Stebbins was killed. When Conningsby arrived in the town he learnt of Stebbins's death, and shortly afterwards he too was murdered and left on the railway tracks. Meanwhile, someone made a thorough search of Mr Stebbins's papers and retrieved the old will.'

'That could have been Conningsby?' suggested Crabb, breaking into Ravenscroft's flow of words.

'Yes, it could have been Conningsby who found the will, and if so that would explain why he was then murdered.

The question is, who stood to benefit from the deaths of Conningsby and the old bookseller?'

'Sir John Critchwood?'

'That would seem to be the obvious solution. The Critchwoods stood to lose everything if the will came to light. But if so, who then killed Sir John — and why? And where is that will now?'

'Mr Critchwood stands to inherit.'

'Yes he does, but why would he kill his own father? He gives the impression that he cares little for his family history, but that of course may be a clever way of eliminating himself from our list of suspects,' said Ravenscroft.

'I cannot believe that he has lived in that house for nearly twenty-five years and knew nothing about either the priest hole or the secret way to the old chapel.'

'Remember that even Travers was surprised by our uncovering of the priest's hiding place, so even he had not been told of its existence.'

'What do we do now, sir?'

'I wonder if we are confusing ourselves with all this past history, and if really the answer to this puzzle is something much more simple and straightforward. Who hated Sir John the most?'

'Troth?'

'Exactly, but did he hate Sir John enough to kill him? If our murderer entered and left by the secret tunnel, then certainly Troth seems the most likely candidate. How did Troth learn about the secret way into Sir John's study? Drive on, Tom. We will pay another visit to our farmer in Charford, but before that I want to call in at the local post office and send a telegram to London. I want to know where exactly Eustace Conningsby came from in London, and whether he is survived by any close relatives.'

* * *

'Would you send this please,' instructed Ravenscroft as he handed over the telegram form.

'Scotland Yard, I see,' smiled the operator.

'Indeed. I am a police officer.'

'I thought you weren't from around these parts.'

'Ledbury.'

'Ledbury? Nice part of the world. I had an uncle who once lived in Ledbury,' began the operator.

'It is urgent. If you could send it as soon as possible I would be most obliged,' interrupted Ravenscroft, laying some coins down on the counter.

'As you wish. I'll have it sent before you can say Merry Christmas — and a very good day to you as well, sir.'

'I have sent the telegram to an old colleague at the Yard,' said Ravenscroft as he and Crabb made their way out of the post office. 'We will see what he can uncover about Eustace Conningsby. I fancy that someone must be missing him by now.'

'They will no doubt be quite distressed to hear of his death,' said Crabb.

'Look out!' exclaimed Ravenscroft as someone ran headlong into him.

'Oh I'm so sorry, sir,' said a young man in uniform.

'Jelps, is it not?' asked Ravenscroft.

'Yes, sir. I'm sorry, sir.'

'You were delivering the post that day when the horse was startled?'

'Yes, sir.'

'You should look where you are going, young man,' said Crabb.

'Yes, sir. Please accept my apologies.'

'Accepted, Jelps. There is no harm done.'

'Thank you, sir,' said Jelps, raising his cap and about to take his leave.

'Of course!' exclaimed Ravenscroft.

'What is it, sir?' asked Crabb.

'Jelps!' called out Ravenscroft. 'A word, if you please.'

'Yes, sir,' said the post boy looking apprehensive as he returned. 'You won't report this to my superior, sir? I've only had this job for the past three months, and I would quite like to retain it. I couldn't help it. It was an accident.'

'No, Jelps, you have nothing to worry about on that score. We are police officers making enquiries in the area. When we had that accident in the lane, with the cab, you said that you had just delivered a letter to Old Dodford Manor. It was on the twenty-third. Do you remember to whom the letter was addressed?'

'It was addressed to Sir John Critchwood.'

'Do you remember what the envelope looked like? Was it a small or large envelope? Could it have been a card inside, or a letter?'

'It was not a card; it was a letter. Quite a small, ordinary envelope.'

'I don't suppose the sender's name was on the outside?'

'I don't recall that being so, sir, but I did notice that it had been posted locally.'

'Good, that is most interesting. When you delivered the letter to Old Dodford Manor, to whom did you give it?'

'Mr March. He said he would give it to Sir John.'

'Thank you, Jelps, you have been most helpful.'

'Glad to have helped.' The post boy gave a cheery smile. 'I am sorry for bumping into you.'

'That is quite alright,' smiled Ravenscroft. 'Just don't make a habit of it.'

'No, sir. I'll look where I am going next time,' replied Jelps.

The two detectives watched as the post boy went on his way.

'I fancy that lad will go far,' remarked Ravenscroft. 'Tom, do you remember when we last interviewed Sir John? He seemed quite unsettled. He was reading a letter when we entered the room. I think he had just received some bad news. I wonder what the letter said? I think we may have been looking at this case from the wrong direction.'

'I don't quite understand you, sir,' said Crabb, perplexed.

'Well, we have been concentrating on what happened on the night Sir John was killed, and what followed on afterwards, when in fact the answer might be found in what happened before.'

'Forgive me, but I still don't see.'

'Sir John receives a letter. He is clearly disturbed by its contents. Later that evening someone kills him. What happened in between? I think we need to know what was in that letter.'

'What about Troth? Could he have sent the letter?'

'Perhaps, but before we visit the farmer, I think we will just call in at the station and see how our prisoner is faring. After a spell in the cells, Spanswick may now be more inclined to talk.'

* * *

'What do you mean Spanswick has escaped?' Ravenscroft stood over Roberts, who was seated on a chair, clutching a blood-stained handkerchief to his head.

'I went down to the cells about an hour ago to take the prisoner a drink,' said Roberts mournfully. 'He was stretched out on his bunk, crying that he was in great pain. I opened the cell door to attend to him. The next thing is, he is on me, and then he knocked me out cold. He must have used my keys to unlock the doors and make good his escape.'

'Good God, man, didn't you think he would do something like this?' Ravenscroft was exasperated. 'We leave one of the most wanted criminals in the whole country in your custody, and you let him go.'

'I am very sorry, sir. I wasn't to know the prisoner would attempt something like that.'

'I am going to be made a laughingstock at the Yard when they learn that we had him in custody and then let him escape. Good heavens, Roberts, what made you fall for a trick like this?'

'I really thought he was dying,' said Roberts, still clutching his head.

'This is the last thing I need. Don't you realise that you may have let a three-time murderer escape? What have you done about recapturing Spanswick?'

'Nothing, sir.'

'What do you mean, "nothing"!'

'I only came round about ten minutes ago.'

'That means he has a head start on us,' said Crabb. 'Shall we go to the railway station to see if he has left the town that way?'

'That is too obvious. We are dealing with a very clever man. He knows that the train station is the first place we will look for him. He could be miles away by now. All we can do is put out an alert and telegraph nearby police stations to keep a lookout for him. This will not look good, Roberts. I don't think Inspector Bullman will be well pleased with you.'

'No, sir.'

'Never mind, we were all young constables once I suppose,' said Ravenscroft, adopting a calmer, resigned tone. 'You had better get yourself seen to by a doctor as soon as possible.'

'I will be better in a minute, sir. I don't want to make a fuss.'

'Is there no one else in the station?'

'Constable Masters should be on duty in ten minutes.'

'Right, then, Roberts, this is what I want you to do. When Constable Masters has arrived, tell him what has happened, and send him to the railway station to see if Spanswick has left the town. We must try all avenues, I suppose, but I don't hold much hope. Then lock up the station, and get yourself seen to. That is an order.'

'Yes, sir.'

'We will be over at Old Dodford Manor. We will be back later.'

* * *

'Good afternoon to you again, Travers,' said Ravenscroft, standing at the entrance to Old Dodford Manor. 'I need a word with Mr March.'

'I believe he is in Sir John's downstairs study, sir.'

Ravenscroft and Crabb followed Travers to the study.

'Good afternoon, Mr March,' said the detective.

'Ravenscroft.' March stood up from his seat behind the large desk. 'I am just in the process of tidying up Sir John's papers.'

'That is what we wish to see you about. I believe that shortly before we visited Sir John in his study here, you took receipt of a letter from the post boy?'

'That is correct.' March looked somewhat perplexed by Ravenscroft's line of questioning.

'Can you describe to us what happened after you took possession of this letter?'

'Well, I came in here and handed it to Sir John.'

'Did you see Sir John open the letter?'

'No, I merely handed the letter to him, and then went back into the hall. Shortly afterwards you arrived and I showed you in here.'

'Mr Travers, perhaps you were you in the room when Sir John opened the letter?' asked Ravenscroft addressing the footman.

'No, sir.'

'Could either of you tell us what transpired after we left the house?'

'Sir John told me he was going out on urgent business, and would I ask the stable lad to bring round his carriage to the front of the building,' said Travers.

'I see. That is most interesting. How did Sir John seem when he went out?'

'He looked very annoyed.'

'Did he say where he was going?'

'No, but I could see that something had upset him.'

'Did you accompany him on his journey?'

'No.'

'Do you usually go out with your master?'

'Yes.'

'But not on this occasion?'

'That is correct, Inspector.'

'Why was that?'

'I don't know. He just said that he only needed the stable lad to go with him.'

'I see. How long was Sir John absent?'

'Sir John was away for just over an hour.'

'Did he say where he had been, or pass any other remarks, when he returned?'

'No. He just went into his study, and said that he was not to be disturbed for the rest of the afternoon, until his guests arrived.'

'Thank you, Travers. I wonder if you would be so kind to go and fetch the stable lad and bring him back here,' requested Ravenscroft.

'Certainly,' replied the footman as he left the room.

'Now, Mr March, it is imperative that we find the letter that Sir John received on that day. You say that you have begun to tidy your master's papers.'

'Yes, but I only began about ten minutes before you arrived.'

'Do you recall seeing such a letter?'

'No, but I have been putting these invoices in order.'

'Then I would be obliged if you would permit Sergeant Crabb and myself to go through these papers.'

'If you insist.'

'Thank you.'

For the next few minutes the two detectives made their way through the collection of papers.

'There appears to be nothing here,' remarked Ravenscroft. 'Try the drawers of the desk, Crabb. Mr March, might Sir John have discarded the letter?'

'That is possible, in which case it would have been placed in the basket over there.'

'I see that it is empty now.'

'Yes, the maid usually empties it twice a day.'

'What happens to these papers and letters that are discarded?'

'We usually burn them in the stove in the kitchen.'

'That is unfortunate.'

'There is nothing in the desk,' said Crabb.

'I suppose Sir John may have taken the letter with him, and later destroyed it,' Ravenscroft sighed.

The door of the study opened and Travers entered, followed by the stable boy.

'This is Stedman, the stable boy,' said Travers.

'Yes, we have met already. Stedman, you may remember that we visited Sir John on the day before his death,' began Ravenscroft.

'Yes, sir.'

'Shortly after we departed, Sir John asked you to bring his carriage round to the front of the house.'

'That is correct.'

'We believe that you accompanied him on the journey he undertook? Where did Sir John ask you to take him?' asked Ravenscroft, suddenly aware that the boy's answers might be providing him with the vital information he needed to solve the case.

'He asked me to take him to the church in Bromsgrove.'

'What happened when you arrived?'

'Sir John asked me to stop just near the bottom of the church steps.'

'Go on,' said Ravenscroft encouragingly.

'Sir John got out of the carriage and asked me to wait. He walked up the steps towards the church.'

'Did he meet with anyone?'

'I gather he was meeting someone there, sir, but he did not say who.'

'How long was he gone?'

'I would say that he was gone for around ten minutes, sir.'

'When he returned did he say anything?'

'Nothing, sir, but I could tell that he was quite annoyed. Oh yes, he did mutter something when he climbed into the carriage.'

'Try to remember what he said.'

'Something like "the blackguard won't get the better of me" or something like that.'

'That is very interesting. Did he say anything else?'

'No, sir.'

'Then you returned home?'

'Yes, sir.'

'So you cannot tell us who it was that Sir John met?' asked Ravenscroft, disappointed.

'I'm sorry, sir.'

'Never mind, you have done well. Before you go, I want you to think very hard before you answer the next question. While you were waiting for Sir John in the carriage at the foot of the steps, did you see anyone either going up or down them?'

'No, sir.'

'And there was no one else standing around in the vicinity?'

'No, sir.'

'Well, thank you, Stedman, you may go.'

The stable boy started to leave the room, then stopped. 'Oh, there was one thing, sir. As we were leaving, we passed a cart further along the road. The horse was tied up, as if the owner expected to return shortly.'

'Had you seen this horse and cart before?'

'Oh yes. I've seen it quite a few times around the town.'

'Do you know who owns this horse and cart?'

'Yes, sir.'

'Well, who is it?' asked Ravenscroft eagerly.

CHAPTER TWELVE

BROMSGROVE

'Now then, men, we must act quickly in case our suspect attempts to destroy any vital evidence,' said Ravenscroft, addressing the group of police officers. 'As soon as we enter, I want you, Roberts, to go to the back of the premises. Search the stables and pay particular attention to the horse-drawn cart. You are looking for anything with bloodstains on it.'

'Yes, sir,' replied the constable.

'Masters, I want you to go to the bedroom and make a thorough search. See if there any bloodstains on the floor that may have been covered up. Sergeant Crabb will search the suspect's private quarters to see if the missing will can be found. I will keep the suspect engaged so that you will not be obstructed in your endeavours. Time is of the essence. Is everything understood?'

The others signified their agreement.

'Then follow me.'

Ravenscroft pushed open the front door of the Black Cross.

'Good morning to you, Inspector,' said Mr Symonds, coming forward to meet the policemen. He looked startled to see so many of them.

'Right, men, set to work,' instructed Ravenscroft.

'I don't understand,' began the landlord, staring anxiously as the policemen went off quickly in all directions.

'All will become clear, Mr Symonds. In the meantime you will oblige me by answering some more questions,' said Ravenscroft, adopting a serious tone.

'Ah well, that all depends on whether I am able to answer such questions. Questions are notoriously difficult things to answer you know,' said Symonds, smiling.

'Sit down there, Symonds,' said Ravenscroft sternly.

The landlord said nothing as he complied with the request.

'Now then, Symonds, I will come straight to the point — can you tell me again about the last time you saw Eustace Conningsby?' asked Ravenscroft, seating himself in a chair at the other side of the table.

'Ah well now let me see. Yes, it was about eleven o'clock. The good gentleman was standing right over there by the fire, warming himself, then he went out through that door, and I never saw him again, to be sure.'

'Well Mr Symonds, I have to tell you that I don't believe a word of it. I don't believe that Conningsby left this inn at all that night. Shall I tell you what I believe really happened? I think you were searching through poor Conningsby's effects, to see what you could take for yourself, when you came across a certain will. Then Conningsby caught you in the act. There was a struggle, and you killed him.' Ravenscroft leant forwards with a look of determination in his eyes.

'Well now, that is a fine tale. What would I be a-wanting with the poor man's possessions?' answered Symonds, unruffled.

'I think you make it a point to search your guests' rooms, while they are here, to see what you can steal, while spreading all those fancy tales about ghostly cavaliers and milkmaids. I think it was you who was in my bedroom the night I was here, trying to see what you could find amongst my possessions, until I woke up and you had to exit quickly. Is that what you were doing when Conningsby caught you in the act?'

'This is a very fine tale, to be sure it is.'

'Yes, Masters?' said Ravenscroft, observing the constable enter the bar.

The policeman came forward and whispered in Ravenscroft's ear.

'That is excellent news, Constable Masters. Thank you. I suggest you now go and assist Sergeant Crabb with his search.'

'Yes, sir,' said the constable, leaving the room.

'Well, Symonds, do you still deny that you killed Conningsby?' asked Ravenscroft.

'Ah well, this is all nonsense, to be sure it is.'

'How do you explain the bloodstains on the floor that my constable has just uncovered underneath a rug in Room 2, the room that Conningsby and myself both occupied,' announced Ravenscroft.

'Ah now, that will be from a guest that was staying here last month. I remember now that he must have cut himself rather badly while he was shaving, the poor man, as he asked for a plaster to cover up the cut. He must have placed the rug over the bloodstains to conceal them, yes that is what he must have done.'

'Did he not tell you that there were bloodstains on the floor?'

'Well now, I do not think that he did, otherwise we would have scrubbed the floor.'

'Nonsense! That is Conningsby's blood on the floor I am sure of it. You thought you would just cover it up with the rug until the stain faded away. Your laziness will prove to be your undoing.'

'That is all very well, inspector, but I do not think that you can prove any of this fanciful tale. They are just bloodstains,' replied the landlord haughtily.

The door opened and Roberts walked into the room holding a linen sheet.

'Yes, Roberts, what did you find?' asked Ravenscroft without taking his eyes off his suspect.

'I found this blood-stained sheet in the stables, sir. It was concealed behind a pile of stacked wood in the corner,' said the constable, laying the item down on the table between the two men.

'Well done, Roberts, excellent work,' said Ravenscroft. 'So, what have you to say about this, Symonds?' he asked, examining the bloodstains on the sheet.

'So that is where that has gone to. The horse cut his leg a few weeks ago in the stable yard, and I used that old sheet to stop the flow and to wipe up the blood until the veterinary man arrived. I had quite intended to burn it on the fire, but then I forgot. I must have pushed it behind the logs waiting to be burnt. It just goes to show that in time everything that is lost will turn up in the most unusual places, usually when you are at least expecting it. My old grandmother in Galway used to say that a lost kitten will always come home to its own mother, if you have the patience to wait for its return.'

'Stop this nonsense!' shouted Ravenscroft, banging his first down hard on the table. 'I know that you killed Conningsby in that bedroom, and that you then used one of the sheets from the bed to wrap up the body. I then think that when no one was looking later that night, you carried the body out to the stables and placed it in your cart. You then drove the cart out to the railway line just outside the station at Bromsgrove, where you deposited the body on the track. You thought that the early-morning train in the dark would be unable to see the corpse on the track, and that it would run over it, thus disfiguring the body so that no one would be able to trace it back to you. But the early-morning trains were cancelled that day, due to signal failures further down the line. I have no doubt that if we search long enough we will be able to find the weapon you used to strike Conningsby on the back of his head.'

Symonds said nothing for a few seconds before speaking. 'Well now, Inspector, this is a very interesting and imaginative narrative, to be sure it is, but you will have the devil of a job to prove it, you know.'

'I have this sheet, and the bloodstains on the floor,' answered Ravenscroft with confidence. 'They are more than enough to secure your conviction, you can be sure of that.'

'That you have, but they mean nothing, as I believe you know.'

Ravenscroft was just about to question his suspect further when the door opened and Crabb and Masters strode into the room.

'We found this, sir. It was stuffed behind some books in Mr Symonds's private quarters,' said Crabb passing over an old document to Ravenscroft.

'"The Last Will and Testament of Sir Edmund Conningsby." So this was what you killed Eustace Conningsby for.'

'I have never seen that document before in all my life,' protested the landlord.

'I have no doubt that this will was made by Sir Edmund Conningsby shortly before his death, and that it names a member of the Conningsby family as his heir, in preference to his daughter Maud Conningsby and her husband Alan Critchwood. Somehow the will disappeared before it could be registered and proved. You realised that if this will came to light now the Critchwoods stood to lose everything, so you wrote to Sir John telling him that you were in possession of the document, and instructing him to meet you at a prescribed time, at the top of the steps of St John's Church in Bromsgrove.'

'How do you know all this?' asked Symonds, who had been somewhat agitated by the production of this last piece of evidence.

'Your cart and horse were seen by Sir John's stable lad near the steps leading up to the church. I think Sir John agreed to pay you a sum of money in return for the will, and told you that if you were to come to his study later that night, after ten o'clock, using the secret tunnel that ran from the old chapel, the deal would be concluded. I think I am correct in that assumption. But what I want to know is what happened next. Why did you decide to kill Sir John and make it look like suicide? You might as well tell us everything Symonds,' said Ravenscroft, knowing that if he pressed hard enough his suspect would be on the point of confessing.

'I am sure I don't know what you are talking about,' protested Symonds defiantly.

'Stop it!' shouted Ravenscroft, again banging the desk. 'We have the blood-stained sheet, the stains on the floor, the old will, and the witness statement that confirms your meeting with Sir John. For goodness' sake, man, can't you see that it is all over with you?'

Symonds let out a deep sigh, wriggled uneasily in his chair and looked down at the floor.

'Come on, man!' demanded Ravenscroft.

'I will tell you the truth, but it is not as you describe it,' said Symonds reluctantly after a few seconds had elapsed.

'Go on,' urged Ravenscroft, as Crabb took out his pocketbook. 'We are all listening.'

'Conningsby caught me in the bedroom. He went mad when he saw me. He attacked me. I had to defend myself. That is all I did. He fell and hit his head on the fireplace. It was an accident. When I looked down at his body on the floor and saw that he was not moving I did not know what to do. Then I thought that if I wrapped up the body in the bed sheet, I could dispose of it on the railway line, and no one would be any the wiser.'

'And the will?'

'I read the will, and I thought that Sir John would be interested in purchasing it, so I wrote to him and asked him to meet me outside the church. He agreed to pay me one hundred pounds, but said that he did not have the money on his person at that time. He said that if I came in secret to his study that night, at ten thirty, he would give me the money in exchange for the will. He told me to use the secret way from the old chapel, so that no one could witness our transaction. So, later that night I went to the chapel, and followed the tunnel, which came up into Sir John's study. When I arrived, there he was waiting for me, but I could see that he had no intention of paying me the money. The old man wanted to cheat me, saying he had no money, and unless I handed over the will straight away, he would see that I was brought up before the justices the following morning. When I told him that I still wanted my money, he became angry, opened the drawer of his desk and took out his pistol, saying he was going to shoot me, and that my body would be thrown into the tunnel, where it would never be found — but I was too quick for him and in the struggle the gun went off. I did not mean to kill him. I had to defend myself, or he would have seen me dead first. You must see that,' pleaded the Irishman. 'I was only acting to defend myself.'

'This is all very interesting, Symonds, but I have to tell you that I don't believe a word of it. I think you found that will and realised that there was money to be made out of it, but first you had to eliminate poor Conningsby and get rid of the body. Then when Sir John told you he had no money, you became angry and searched through his drawers, where you saw the gun and shot him in a violent rage. Then you decided to stage a suicide. You locked the door from the inside and retraced your steps to the old chapel, closing the panelled entrance and pushing the bookcase against the opening in the chapel.' Ravenscroft stared hard at his suspect.

'I have told you what happened.'

'Well we shall have to see what the jury thinks. I also think you killed Mr Stebbins, the bookseller, because you knew he had the will, but before you could return to make a search of his premises, Conningsby arrived and recovered the document before you.'

'Well now, Inspector, you have all that wrong, and I thought you were an intelligent man. I had nothing to do with the old bookseller's killing. The first time I saw that will was amongst Conningsby's possessions, and that is God's truth, on my mother's honour. I had nothing to do with the old man's murder.'

Ravenscroft said nothing as he leaned back in his chair.

'You have to believe me. I never killed the old book-seller. I never meant to kill either Conningsby or Sir John. It was all an accident.'

'Put the cuffs on him, Crabb. Roberts, Masters, take the prisoner to the station.'

* * *

'Well Ravenscroft you certainly have been very busy,' said Detective Inspector Bullman, as he sat at the table in the back room of the station, later that afternoon, with Ravenscroft and Crabb.

'I have Symonds's signed confession here,' said Ravenscroft. 'He still maintains that he was compelled to kill both men in order to defend himself. I maintain that he killed Conningsby in order to secure possession of the will, and that he then shot Sir John because the old man refused to hand over the money.'

'That was a very clever trick, making it look like suicide and locking the door from the inside. He had me fooled there,' admitted Bullman. 'It was fortunate that you found that secret tunnel to the old chapel. That was good police work, Ravenscroft.'

'I knew there had to be another way in which Sir John had been killed. I never believed for one moment that he committed suicide. It was not in his character. I have read the will, and it was indeed made by Sir Edmund Conningsby a few weeks before he died. He completely disowned his daughter, Maud, on account of her marriage to Alan Critchwood, and left everything to his late brother's son, a certain Rupert Conningsby. I don't know what happened to the will after Edmund's death, but it certainly wasn't proved. My guess is that it got mixed up with a lot of other papers, where it remained for over a hundred and fifty years, until it came into the possession of Mr Stebbins the bookseller. He undoubtedly realised its worth and somehow managed to track down Rupert Conningsby's descendant, Eustace Conningsby, who apparently resided in London. He then corresponded with Conningsby and told him to come to Bromsgrove where he would "gain something to his advantage", but before that happened, Mr Stebbins was killed.'

'So what happened when Eustace Conningsby arrived in town?' asked Bullman.

'He learnt that Stebbins had been killed the week before, but then thought that he might obtain the will by searching through the dead man's papers. He was successful, and took it back with him to the Black Cross, where he was cruelly killed by Mr Symonds,' answered Ravenscroft. 'The evidence of the blood-stained floorboards, the sheet in which he wrapped the body, the testimony of the stable lad, and the fact that this will was found in his possession, should be more than enough to convict the man.'

'So all this stuff you mentioned about Sir John trying to buy up Troth's land so he could build more houses in the town was completely irrelevant to the case.'

'Indeed it was.'

'What about this Bromsgrove Gas Light and Coke Company?'

'It had nothing to do with his death.'

'Hum, pity about that Spanswick fellow. You should have put an armed guard on him,' said Bullman, pulling a miserable face.

'The station was rather short-staffed, and Roberts is only a junior constable. He will learn in time. It could have happened to any of us when we were young.'

'That's as may be. It just doesn't look good, though. It reflects badly on us and makes us look a bit of a laughing-stock with our colleagues down at the Yard.'

'I sent Constable Masters to the railway station, and apparently a man of Spanswick's description was seen earlier boarding the afternoon train to Birmingham. By the time we alerted the local police there, it was too late. The train had already arrived at its destination. Nevertheless I have asked the Birmingham police to post a description of Spanswick in the area.'

'Too late, Ravenscroft,' interrupted Bullman. 'He will be miles away by now.'

'I fear you are right,' Ravenscroft sighed.

'Still, your apprehension of a double killer must have done the station some good in the eyes of the powers that be. You might as well go home now, Ravenscroft. I'll see this matter through.' Bullman rose to his feet. 'You have done more than enough to clear up this case.'

'There is still the matter of Mr Stebbins's murder,' protested Ravenscroft.

'Why? You don't think that this Symonds fellow killed him as well?'

'No, I don't believe that he did. I think that the first time he saw the will was in the bedroom of the Black Cross, when it was in Eustace Conningsby's possession.'

'I thought you would come round to my way of thinking. That lad killed Mr Stebbins and no mistake. He thought his uncle was going to lend him that money, and when the old man refused, he killed him in a fit of anger because he had been spited.'

'I still don't think that he did it. I have known the lad for nearly six years, and I don't believe that he would have done such a thing. It is not in his nature.'

'You are letting sentimentality cloud your judgement, Ravenscroft. That is always a dangerous thing. One has to stay objective in these matters. You might as well admit it, you have no other suspects.'

'I am convinced that it must have been someone that Mr Stebbins loaned money too.'

'He loaned money to half the town of Bromsgrove at one time or another. Why, I even borrowed some money from him earlier this year, but that does not mean that I murdered him because I could not afford to pay him back,' laughed Bullman.

'Why did you borrow money from Stebbins?' asked Ravenscroft.

'I was moving house at the time, and had some bills to pay. I just wanted the money to tide me over for a while. There was nothing more to it, as I am sure it was with all those other people he lent money to.'

'I suppose you're right, Bullman,' admitted Ravenscroft somewhat reluctantly.

'Let justice take its course, that's what I say. That lad will stand trial at the end of the week, and if he is found guilty, as I am sure he will be, he will surely hang. There is nothing you can do about it. You have done your best, but these things are inevitable. The lad is guilty. Go home, Ravenscroft, and enjoy what is left of the festive season with your family and friends.'

CHAPTER THIRTEEN

27 DECEMBER

The prisoner looked through the bars of his cell into the courtyard, and watched the flakes of snow gently falling on to the ground as the dawn was breaking, knowing that he would probably never see the sun rise again.

Ravenscroft had promised that he would return to save him, but he now realised that he had been deceived and that his last hope had been dashed.

The cell door opened.

'It's time, Stebbins,' said a voice, both compassionate and final in its tone.

He turned round to face the governor, the jailer, the guard and the priest, wondering why the time had gone so quickly since they had given him that early-morning breakfast, and why they had now sent so many to occupy the tiny cell.

'Come, Stebbins,' instructed the governor.

'I didn't do it,' he protested, but his voice was weak. No one would believe his pitiful entreaties.

The jailer opened the door once more, and moved to one side of the cell in order that the priest might form the head of the procession.

The guard reached out for his arm and indicated that it was time for him to take his place. He looked wistfully around the cell that had been his home for the past two weeks, and felt a cold sickening in his stomach.

The procession moved off slowly, the priest at its head reading aloud from the Bible, then the prisoner escorted by the guard, and finally the governor. As they walked down the cold dank corridor he found himself counting the steps and looking at the moisture clinging to the sides of the walls, and hoping that even at this late hour his saviour would finally come and set him free.

Then there were the steps to climb, and the door at the end of the flight, with another guard waiting for his arrival.

The door opened and he followed the priest into the airless and unholy room.

Then he saw the hangman standing by the trap, and his knees gave way as the full realisation of what was about to happen to him swept over him like a wave that could not be turned — and he slipped without resistance towards the floor.

'Have courage, lad,' said someone as he was pulled back on to his feet and urged to step nearer to the allotted space.

'Have you anything to say?' asked the priest.

He nodded his head. What could they expect him to say?

'There is still time to confess your sins, my son. Jesus will always give salvation to a sinner who accepts that he has transgressed, and asks for his eternal forgiveness at the gates of heaven,' said the priest, smiling gently after he had uttered the words.

'But I didn't do it. I didn't kill my uncle,' he pleaded in a voice that was scarcely more than a whisper.

'Repent, my son. No good will come of this denial. You must see that.'

'Where is Inspector Ravenscroft? He said he would save me.'

'Who is this Ravenscroft?' asked the governor.

'A policeman,' mumbled the jailer.

'He said he would save me,' cried the prisoner.

'I am sorry, Stebbins, but there is no last-minute reprieve,' said the governor. 'You should do as the priest advises, and make peace with your maker.'

'No, no! This is not right!' he called out, summoning up his last ounce of courage.

The governor nodded in the direction of the hangman, and that was the last sight he saw as he felt only the blackness and suffocation of the bag as it was pulled over his head.

'No! No!' he called out, but he knew that no one would hear his words.

Then he felt the rope being placed around his neck.

'You said that you would save me!'

'God have mercy on your soul, my son.'

He felt a sudden pain as the floor gave way beneath his feet — and then there was only oblivion.

Oh, why hadn't Ravenscroft come to save him?

He had promised.

He had deserted him in his last hour of need.

The book!

If only Ravenscroft had looked in the book!

* * *

'Samuel! Samuel!'

'No! No!' cried out Ravenscroft.

'Samuel, wake up!' said a voice calling out to him in the distance, as though it came from the end of a long dark tunnel.

'No! No, you can't execute him. He is innocent, I tell you!'

'Execute who?'

'Stebbins. I must save Stebbins. I have got to save Stebbins!'

'It is alright now, Samuel. It is over.'

'Where am I?' asked Ravenscroft, looking anxiously around the bedroom.

'You are at home, in your bed,' said Lucy.

'I must have had a bad dream.'

'You were calling out in your sleep.'

'Oh, I'm sorry to have woken you, my dear.' Ravenscroft struggled upright, wiping perspiration away from his eyes.

'You are very hot. I trust that you are not sickening for something. Here, drink this.' Lucy poured out a glass of water from the flagon on the bedside table.

'Thank you.' Ravenscroft sipped the reviving liquid. 'What time is it?'

'It is still quite dark.'

'I had the most terrible dream. I dreamt that they were hanging poor Stebbins. He was still professing his innocence, but no one was prepared to listen to him. He kept calling out that I would come to save him before the hangman would put the noose around his neck, but the worst of it was that I was not there. I could not save him, Lucy. It was all so terrible. I could do nothing.'

'Don't distress yourself, Samuel. It was only a dream,' said Lucy.

'Yes I know, but don't you see — it is a dream that will come true. In just two days from now Stebbins will stand trial, and if he is found guilty he will hang — and I have done nothing to save him.'

'I am sure you have done everything you can, and I know you will speak up for him at the trial. The jury will no doubt look favourably upon him, and he may yet go free.'

'You don't really believe that, do you?'

'What about this man Symonds, are you sure that he did not kill Mr Stebbins to get his hands on that will?' suggested Lucy.

'No. He would never have known that the bookseller was in possession of such a document at that time. No, the first time he saw the will was when he came across it amongst Eugene Conningsby's possessions. Symonds killed both Conningsby and Sir John, there is no doubt about it; but I also know that he did not kill Mr Stebbins.'

'Then who did? I don't like those Nightingales, from what you have told me about them. You said that the Trollope novel had been taken by Peter Nightingale from the bookshelves.'

'Yes, but I do not think that he would have murdered Mr Stebbins just to acquire another book to add his collection. It is not even a particularly valuable book.'

'What about his sister, Mary Nightingale? You are convinced that she is having an affair with young Mr Critchwood. They could have planned all the murders together.'

'You mean they killed old Stebbins and Conningsby in order to obtain the will, and then Christopher killed his own father to inherit the title — but you are forgetting that Symonds has already confessed to the two murders.'

'No, I suppose you are right, but I still don't like them. I think they are up to no good. What about your Detective Inspector Bullman? He has not exactly been very helpful to you in your investigations, and seems more than anxious to see that Stebbins is found guilty. Did you ask him what his name was doing in old Mr Stebbins's book?'

'No, in fact he volunteered the information. He said he was moving house at that time, and wanted to borrow the money to see him through until his next salary arrived. It appears as though the old bookseller loaned money to half the population of Bromsgrove.'

'Then you and Tom must go back there tomorrow and make more enquiries. I know that if there is an answer to be found, you and Tom will find it. I have every confidence in you. You must not give up.'

'Yes, that is all we can do, and pray that we find something.' Ravenscroft took another sip of water.

'Try to get some sleep until the morning,' said Lucy.

'Yes of course. I'm sorry to have wakened you.' Ravenscroft lay down once more and drew the counterpane up under his chin.

'Sleep, Samuel,' urged Lucy.

Ravenscroft sighed and looked up at the shadows on the ceiling. Why had this case been so difficult? What had he missed? Then he saw again the faces of Peter and Mary Nightingale, of Travers and March, Doctor Fortescue and Lowbeam the solicitor, Spanswick and Troth, Christopher Critchwood and Inspector Bullman. Had one of these people killed old Mr Stebbins — and if so, which one — and why? Whatever the answers, he knew that he had to save Stebbins — and he was more than aware that time was running out.

Then his thought turned back to the dream. What did Stebbins say as they hanged him? "The book! If only Ravenscroft had looked in the book!" What did he mean? What book? Mr Stebbins's account book? But surely he had looked there already?

* * *

'Good morning, Tom,' said Lucy as Crabb entered the drawing room the following morning.

'Good morning to you, Mrs Ravenscroft.'

'Can we offer you some tea?'

'No thank you, Mrs Ravenscroft,' replied Crabb. 'I've already had breakfast.'

'You must excuse my husband for not speaking to you, Tom, but he has been studying that book intently for the past two hours, and consulting a number of volumes on the shelves.'

'Oh, I'm sorry, Tom,' said Ravenscroft, without looking up from the book before him on the breakfast table.

'That is the old bookseller's account book?' asked Crabb.

'It is indeed,' replied Ravenscroft.

'He had a terrible dream in the night,' said Lucy.

'Oh, I'm sorry to hear that.'

'I think I have it, Tom.' Ravenscroft suddenly closed the book with such force that the vibration was in danger of damaging the teacups on the table.

'I knew you would,' said Lucy, recovering her composure.

'It was silly how we missed it.' Ravenscroft jumped up from his chair. 'We have been looking at this case from entirely the wrong angle. Come on, Tom, there is not a moment to lose if we are to save young Stebbins and apprehend the real criminal. If we are quick, we might catch the nine fifteen.'

'Right, sir,' said Crabb, as Ravenscroft took hold of the book and strode out of the room, pausing only momentarily to retrieve his coat and hat from the hallstand.

'When will you be back?' called out Lucy, following the men into the hallway — but the door had already closed behind the two detectives.

* * *

'You see, Tom, I realised this morning that we had been looking in the wrong place for old Mr Stebbins's killer,' said Ravenscroft, as he and Crabb sat in the railway carriage on its way to Bromsgrove. 'When we first found this account book, I assumed that the killer must have been someone to whom the bookseller had recently loaned money, and who had no desire to pay it back. That is why I only looked at the entries on the last few pages, which list transactions over the past year or two. Many names appeared, some like Bullman and Nightingale, who borrowed small amounts, who had either repaid their debts or were on the point of doing so when the moneylender was killed. Then there were people like Sir John Critchwood who borrowed larger amounts to either invest in business ventures or pay off other debtors.'

'Yes, sir, I understand that,' said a puzzled Crabb, wondering what his superior officer was about to reveal.

'Then today I thought maybe the answer might be hidden further back in this account book. The first entry was made over twenty years ago, and no doubt some of the people he then lent money to have then since died. What if there was someone who borrowed money almost on a regular basis over the years, a person who managed to repay some of the loans, but was always asking for more money, and consequently increasing his debt to the old man? That is when I began to study the pages in more detail, and there was one name that stood out more than any others.' Ravenscroft opened the book and pointing to a number of entries on one of the pages.

'Good Lord!' exclaimed Crabb. 'But that does not seem possible.'

'Then I looked at the dates when the money had been borrowed, and noticed that on the occasions when it had been repaid, with interest of course, it was usually only two or three days after the loan had been taken out.'

'So the money could not have been used to repay other loans, or to be invested in business enterprises?'

'Exactly! The person who took out these loans was obviously a gambler. Then I checked with my reference books at home, and found that each of the loans had been taken out a day before one of the important annual race meetings at Worcester. This entry here was taken out one day before the Worcester Stakes; this one before Gold Cup Day, and so on. Sometimes our borrower won and repaid his debt the following day, but more often than not he lost, and the debt was not repaid. In these pages, over the years, the overall debt steadily mounts, until it eventually disappears altogether.'

'Oh, why do you think that happened, sir?'

'Either the debtor came into money and repaid the loan, or the debt was replaced by something else, which possibly caused more hardship. I think I know which.'

'So how are we to proceed further?' asked Crabb.

'It is one thing deducing who, and why, this murder took place, but it will be another matter trying to prove it. We need to act carefully if we are to extract a confession, but before that our evidence must be watertight. There is one person who can provide us with the missing piece in this jigsaw. It is a person we should have interviewed much earlier in this investigation.'

* * *

As the two detectives turned the corner into the passageway that would take them back to the old bookseller's shop, Ravenscroft was rewarded by seeing a familiar figure seated on the ground, an old cap stretched before him in which lay a few copper coins.

'Hello to you, Jonas. How are you today?' asked Ravenscroft.

'Cold,' muttered the old beggar, giving a shiver.

'You remember me and my colleague?'

The beggar strained hard as he looked up at the two figures.

'Why bless you, sir; you gave me that money so that I could have a room for Christmas.'

'Indeed we did, and I trust that you were comfortable?'

'As well as could be expected; it's going to be cold tonight, though. There will be a frost, if I am not mistaken.'

'Well here is another coin for you, to enable you to have a hearty meal, and secure a room for the night.' Ravenscroft reached into his pocket.

'Lord bless you, sir. You is a saint.'

'There is also another coin for you, if you can provide us with some information.'

'Willingly,' replied the beggar eagerly.

'This is your usual place, I believe?'

'Yes, sir. It keeps me out of that draught that blows down the main street. It is real cold out there at times.'

'I fancy you see everyone who comes and goes along here on their way to the courtyard at the rear end?'

'I do, there is no one that escapes my eye.'

'And there is no other way out? Everyone who enters must pass you by when they have finished their business?'

'That is so.'

'You remember old Mr Stebbins, the bookseller at the end of the courtyard?'

'Yes, who could forget that old devil.'

'Did he ever give you money?'

'Never, he was a miserable mean old skinflint. He would not even say good morning to you. He had a face that would curdle milk just by looking at it.'

'We understand that he was in the habit of lending money to people?'

'Yes he did, the silly devils. Nothing good comes of borrowing other people's money.'

'So I suppose quite a few of these people came to the shop over the years?'

'Yes.'

'And you saw them all, as they passed you by on their way to the courtyard?'

'That I did.'

'Do you remember the day the old bookseller was killed? It was about two weeks ago.' asked Ravenscroft, hoping that the old beggar would shortly provide him with the vital information he so desperately needed.

'Yes, all that commotion, the police arriving and taking that lad away. They said that he had gone and knifed the old man. Good for him, I say. He had it coming. The old skinflint won't be missed. I'd shake the lad's hand if I could.'

'Did you see the young lad enter the court a few minutes earlier?'

'I did. He gave me a halfpenny, he did. Good lad, he was.'

'Do you remember anyone else entering the courtyard, shortly after the young lad entered?'

'Yes, there was that Mr Nightingale. He followed the lad in a few minutes later.'

'Good. Now I have a very important question for you to answer. Think hard. Did you see anyone else enter the courtyard, shortly before the young lad?'

The old beggar lowered his head as if in deep thought.

'Well?' asked Ravenscroft after nearly half a minute of silence had elapsed. 'Did you see anyone?'

'No,' replied Jonas shaking his head. 'I didn't see anyone.'

'Perhaps in the hour before the lad went into the courtyard?'

'No, there was no one.'

'You were here for all that time?' asked Ravenscroft.

'I was here for all that afternoon.'

'It was very cold and foggy. Do you think anyone could have slipped past you when you were not looking?' suggested the detective.

'No. I was right here. Everyone has to come past me. If there had been anyone, I would have seen them, wouldn't I?'

'Indeed you would.' Ravenscroft gave a little smile.

'Is that all? You said there would be another coin.'

'Indeed I did.' Ravenscroft reached into his coat pocket once again.

'Thank you, sir. The Lord give you and yours a happy New Year.'

'I thank you, Jonas. I think it will be a very good year indeed.'

* * *

'Good morning to you, Mrs Marquis,' said Ravenscroft as he and Crabb entered the small dressmaker's shop.

'That sounds like a familiar voice, if I am not mistaken,' replied the woman, looking up from her sewing in the corner of the room.

'Inspector Ravenscroft,' announced the detective.

Mrs Marquis smiled as she laid down her sewing. 'I thought as much, and your nice young sergeant as well.'

'I trust I find you well?' asked Ravenscroft.

'As well as an old woman of my age can expect.'

'I have returned because I believe you may be able to help us; in fact you are now the only person who can be of assistance to us.'

'Oh, I would say that all sounds very important, by the tone of your voice.'

'I wanted to ask you about the man you heard on the afternoon of the murder of Mr Stebbins. You said that you heard the sound of heavy boots entering the shop, and also leaving shortly afterwards?'

'Yes, that is so. Have you caught the gentleman yet? If you have, I am afraid that I won't be able to identify him for you. As I explained to you before, my eyesight is not what it was ten years ago.'

'No, Mrs Marquis, we have not caught the man. In fact I am now faced with a terrible situation, and it is only you who can be of assistance to me.'

'I will try my best,' said the old woman smiling.

'The young lad who was arrested, he is the nephew of the Mr Stebbins. I have known him for nearly six years, and I can honestly say that a more honest and faithful young man you would never expect to meet. He has recently married a most industrious and supportive companion, and he and his young wife are seeking to get on in this world. They are both in service, but young Stebbins wants to better his life. He wants to purchase an old building in the town where he resides, so that he and his wife can start a small boarding establishment of their own. That was why he came to see his uncle, to see whether the old man would lend him the money so that his dream might come true. Now all that promise and hope has been dashed. He stands falsely accused of a terrible murder, which he did not commit. He will stand trial next week and will probably be found guilty. Shortly afterwards, he will hang, an innocent man struck down in his youth. His wife and friends will be devastated. I have tried desperately to clear his name, but to no avail. I can do no more. It is not right that this should come to pass, would you not agree, Mrs Marquis?'

The dressmaker said nothing as she turned away, a troubled expression on her face.

'It is a terrible business. This young man had everything to live for, and now he has nothing,' continued Ravenscroft. 'If I could take his place on the scaffold I would do so. It is at times like this that one begins to question one's faith in the justice system, and in everything which is honest and truthful in this world.'

'How did you know?' The old woman's voice was scarcely audible.

'There were no heavy footsteps outside the bookseller's that afternoon. The old beggar has confirmed to us that was the case. It is all in Mr Stebbins's book,' said Ravenscroft. 'There are many names here, over a twenty-year period. Your late husband's name appears many times over the years. The loans were taken out just before race days at Worcester; some were repaid, others not.'

'Mr Marquis was a very foolish and weak man, but he was my husband. There was nothing I could do to prevent his addiction. He always believed that one day he would win so much money that we would be able to leave this dreary courtyard, where the sun never shines and the air is bad, and that we would buy a little cottage in the countryside where we would see out our days, but I knew it was a dream that would never be fulfilled. So he borrowed more and more, until Mr Stebbins said that there was no money available unless he bought us out. So we let him have the shop and the rooms above, in order to cancel out the debt. There was no other way out for us. The old moneylender said that now he owned us we would have to work for him. The strain of it all gradually wore down my poor husband. He was never a well man. He had a frail constitution. The worry of it all contributed to his early death.'

'I am sorry,' sympathised Ravenscroft.

'I thought that after my husband's death it would all stop, and that I would be free, but the wrinkled old man wanted his pound of flesh. He said that I would work for him until the day I died. There would never be an escape. But even that was not enough for him. When my eyes gradually weakened and I could not work as nimbly as I used to do, he said that he wanted more. Then last month he said that at the end of the year I would have to leave. He wanted to sell the shop and the rooms above. I pleaded with him to let me stay until the end of my days, but he said no, I was to leave, and that was that. The man had not an ounce of

Christian charity in his soul. I was desperate; I did not know what to do. I had nowhere to go, you must understand that. This has been my home for the last twenty years. I could not bear to leave. I know to some people that may sound silly, but this little room and the one above is all I have in this lonely world. If I was turned out now I would end my days as a beggar. I am sorry. Will you excuse me if I sit down on this chair?'

'Of course, please take your time, Mrs Marquis.'

'You have no idea what it was like to sit here day after day, looking out of my window, and seeing that dreadful man getting richer and richer at the expense of other people's misfortunes. So on that fateful afternoon I resolved on one last attempt. I would throw myself on his mercy. I crossed over to the shop when it was quiet, and appealed to his better nature to let me stay, but he just laughed in my face, saying I was a useless old woman who was no good to anyone, and that I should have been in my cold grave years ago. Then he made fun of my dear husband, saying he had been a stupid foolish old man who had not an ounce of common sense, and that he should have been put out of his misery years ago. I was so angry. I don't know what came over me. I saw that knife on his desk, and I picked it up and plunged it into his back, two or three times. I did not know what I was doing. I suppose I just wanted to rid this world of such a despicable and uncaring man. I did it for my poor husband. God help me, I did not want to do it, you must believe me.' Her voice faltered as her eyes filled with tears.

'I am sorry,' said Ravenscroft sympathetically, after a few seconds of silence had elapsed. 'I understand, but I am afraid that you will have to come with us. You know that.'

'Yes. Will I see this little room ever again? It is my world, you know. It is all I have.'

'I do not think so.'

'Will you hand me my shawl? I am so sorry for that young man. I did not mean for him to find that body, and for him to be charged with Stebbins's murder. I would have spoken out if they had found him guilty. I would not have let them hang him. You believe that, don't you?'

Ravenscroft said nothing as Crabb placed the shawl round the old lady's shoulders.

'Tell him that I am so sorry for all the distress I have caused him.'

* * *

'So there we have it, Tom,' said Ravenscroft later that day, as he and Crabb walked along the street in Worcester. 'We have solved three murders and apprehended two perpetrators.'

'Most satisfactory,' remarked Crabb.

'One murderer killed for greed, while the other was driven to it by the actions of a mean-spirited man. Much as I sympathise with Mrs Marquis, and feel for her predicament, I fear that she will pay the ultimate price.'

'It is very sad, sir, and at her time of life.'

'See up there, Tom,' said Ravenscroft looking upwards at the sky. 'I do believe the sun is about to make an appearance at long last.'

'I thought the ice was beginning to melt.'

'It is surely a sign of better things to come. It will be good to return home. Ah, here we are.'

Ravenscroft knocked loudly on the jail door.

'Alright! Alright! I'm coming. No need to wake the dead,' said a familiar voice as the great oak door was slowly unlocked. 'Can't a man be left in peace? Oh, it's you again.'

'Good day to you, Mr Smith, I trust you have been taking care of our mutual friend?' said Ravenscroft, smiling.

'I have, and I reckons you owes me a shilling for me pains,' grumbled the jailer.

'Quite so, that was our agreement, and here is the money.' Ravenscroft handed over a coin.

'Thanking you kindly, sir. You'll be a-wanting to see the prisoner again, I expect. He will not be long for this world, so you best make the most of it while you can.'

'That is where you are wrong,' said Ravenscroft. 'This piece of paper gives you the authority to release him forthwith into our safe keeping. The prisoner is innocent of the crime.'

Smith grabbed the paper in question and pretended to read the words.

'It is all in order, I can assure you,' said Ravenscroft.

'Well you best come along with me then, officers,' said Smith grudgingly, before handing the sheet of paper back to Ravenscroft.

'You can also expect two more prisoners tomorrow sent over from the police station in Bromsgrove. One is an elderly lady. I would be obliged if you would show her some kindness.' Ravenscroft handed Smith another coin as the trio made their way down the passageway between the cells.

The jailer unlocked the cell door. 'Stebbins, you is free to go.'

Ravenscroft and Crabb stepped into the cell, as Stebbins rose from his bunk.

'Lord, it's Inspector Ravenscroft, is it not?'

'I have some good news for you Stebbins. I am pleased to say that we have caught the person who murdered your uncle, and obtained a full confession. You are free, Stebbins,' said Ravenscroft, smiling.

'God bless you. I knew that you would not let me down,' said the youth, coming forward, with tears of relief in his eyes. 'I never doubted it for a minute.'

'It was good that your wife contacted us, or this crime would have gone unsolved.'

'Thank you, Inspector Ravenscroft. I knew that you would put things right,' said the grateful youth.

'Let us get out of this place. We all have people waiting for us at home, who will no doubt be very pleased to see us,' said Ravenscroft. 'The rest of the Christmas season is there for all of us to enjoy.'

EPILOGUE

Symonds stood trial for the murders of Eustace Conningsby and Sir John Critchwood. He was found guilty and shortly afterwards was hanged at Worcester Jail.

Alice Marquis was found guilty of the murder of Marcus Stebbins, and sentenced to be hanged. However, owing to her extreme age and frailty, and given the circumstances of her situation, the service was commuted to life imprisonment.

Christopher Critchwood and Mary Nightingale were eventually married.

The wife and heirs of Eustace Conningsby contested the last proved will of Sir Edmund Conningsby, and a lengthy court case ensued, 'Conningsby versus Critchwood', which we understand is still on-going.

Jelps the post boy did well and eventually became the postmaster at Bromsgrove Post Office.

The courtyard which had been the home to old Mr Stebbins and Alice Marquis's shops was eventually demolished.

The Black Cross is still reputed to be haunted by a number of ghosts, although evidence of actual sightings is difficult to come by.

Stebbins eventually inherited a sum of money from his late uncle's estate, with which he and his wife Maisie opened a bed and breakfast establishment in Great Malvern.

There were various sightings of Albert Spanswick, alias Monsieur Hubert, in places as far apart as Birmingham, Manchester, Berlin and Paris, during the following years, but he always evaded apprehension. It is rumoured that a man of his description was last heard of attempting to sell shares in the new Tower Bridge, which is presently under construction in the City of London, but we have been unable to substantiate these claims.

Ravenscroft enjoyed the rest of the festive season in the company of his friends and family.

THE END

ALSO BY KERRY TOMBS

INSPECTOR RAVENSCROFT DETECTIVE MYSTERIES

Book 1: THE MALVERN MURDERS
Book 2: THE WORCESTER WHISPERERS
Book 3: THE LEDBURY LAMPLIGHTERS
Book 4: THE TEWKESBURY TOMB
Book 5: THE DROITWICH DECEIVERS
Book 6: THE PERSHORE POISONERS
Book 7: THE UPTON UNDERTAKERS
Book 8: THE HEREFORDSHIRE HANGMEN
Book 9: THE BROMSGROVE BOOKSELLER

FREE KINDLE BOOKS

Do you love mysteries, historical fiction and romance? Join 1,000s of readers enjoying great books through our mailing list. You'll get new releases and great deals every week from one of the UK's leading independent publishers.

Join today, and you'll get your first bargain book this month!

www.joffebooks.com

Follow us on Facebook, Twitter and Instagram @joffebooks

Thank you for reading this book. If you enjoyed it please leave feedback on Amazon, and if there is anything we missed or you have a question about then please get in touch. The author and publishing team appreciate your feedback and time reading this book.

We're very grateful to eagle-eyed readers who take the time to contact us. Please send any errors you find to corrections@joffebooks.com. We'll get them fixed ASAP.

Printed in Great Britain
by Amazon

67230707R00130